THE C

Nancy knew she should

She should be grateful ___ headed the billion-dollar program that had saved her life and could save so many others.

She should be grateful to her husband, Dr. John Victor, for helping her even though she was having an affair with another man, and for becoming her loving mate again during her painful period of recovery.

She should be grateful to the Tank, the marvelous machine in which her body had lain for six months that so easily could have turned into an eternity.

She should be grateful instead of being so horribly afraid. . . .

SLEEPING BEAUTY

Sensational SIGNET Bestsellers

- [ ] **BRAIN** by Robin Cook. (#AE1260—$3.95)
- [ ] **THE DELTA DECISION** by Wilbur Smith. (#AE1335—$3.50)
- [ ] **CENTURY** by Fred Mustard Stewart. (#AE1407—$3.95)
- [ ] **ORIGINAL SINS** by Lisa Alther. (#AE1448—$3.95)
- [ ] **MAURA'S DREAM** by Joel Gross. (#AE1262—$3.50)
- [ ] **THE DONORS** by Leslie Alan Horvitz and H. Harris Gerhard, M.D. (#AE1338—$2.95)
- [ ] **SMALL WORLD** by Tabitha King. (#AE1408—$3.50)
- [ ] **THE KISSING GATE** by Pamela Haines. (#AE1449—$3.50)
- [ ] **THE CROOKED CROSS** by Barth Jules Sussman. (#AE1203—$2.95)
- [ ] **CITY KID** by Mary MacCracken. (#AE1336—$2.95)
- [ ] **CHARLIES DAUGHTER** by Susan Child. (#AE1409—$2.50)
- [ ] **JUDGMENT DAY** by Nick Sharman. (#AE1450—$2.95)
- [ ] **THE DISTANT SHORE** by Susannah James. (#AE1264—$2.95)
- [ ] **FORGED IN BLOOD** (Americans at War #2) by Robert Leckie. (#AE1337—$2.95)
- [ ] **TECUMSEH** by Paul Lederer. (#AE1410—$2.95)
- [ ] **THE JASMINE VEIL** by Gimone Hall. (#AE1451—$2.95)*

*Prices Slightly Higher in Canada

Buy them at your local bookstore or use this convenient coupon for ordering.
THE NEW AMERICAN LIBRARY, INC.,
P.O. Box 999, Bergenfield, New Jersey 07621
Please send me the books I have checked above. I am enclosing $_____
(please add $1.00 to this order to cover postage and handling). Send check or money order—no cash or C.O.D.'s. Prices and numbers are subject to change without notice.
Name_____
Address_____
City _____ State _____ Zip Code _____
Allow 4-6 weeks for delivery.
This offer is subject to withdrawal without notice.

SLEEPING BEAUTY

by
L. L. Greene

Ⓞ
A SIGNET BOOK
NEW AMERICAN LIBRARY
TIMES MIRROR

PUBLISHED BY
THE NEW AMERICAN LIBRARY
OF CANADA LIMITED

For Norman

NAL BOOKS ARE AVAILABLE AT QUANTITY DISCOUNTS
WHEN USED TO PROMOTE PRODUCTS OR SERVICES. FOR
INFORMATION PLEASE WRITE TO PREMIUM MARKETING
DIVISION, THE NEW AMERICAN LIBRARY, INC., 1633
BROADWAY, NEW YORK, NEW YORK 10019.

First Printing, June, 1982

  2 3 4 5 6 7 8 9

 SIGNET TRADEMARK REG. U.S. PAT. OFF. AND FOREIGN COUNTRIES
REGISTERED TRADEMARK - MARCA REGISTRADA
HECHO EN WINNIPEG, CANADA

SIGNET, SIGNET CLASSICS, MENTOR, PLUME, MERIDIAN
and NAL BOOKS are published in Canada by The New American
Library of Canada, Limited, Scarborough, Ontario

PRINTED IN CANADA
COVER PRINTED IN U.S.A.

1

You're too smart to die, Nancy Seymour thought. Sometimes she was positive that the whole thing was a ghastly mistake. That someone else's blood sample had been switched with hers. Other times she suspected an evil prank, or a blown circuit somewhere in the bowels of the Great Computer. Perhaps a cure would be found at the last minute. The doctors agreed it was possible. Then she lined up the arguments on her side and weighed them. On the days she felt better, they would make a great deal of sense. But soon time will start running out, she realized; then we'll see what you're really made of.

The elevator door slid open. Nancy stepped out, directly into the sixth-floor newsroom of NBC Rockefeller Center. She found herself smiling. The best trick she knew was not allowing for time to stop and think. A newsroom was the perfect place for that. Within half a dozen steps she had become completely immersed in the familiar bedlam. Every teletype machine on the floor was running full blast. Bells rang and keys pounded like hail on a tin roof as the cranky machines spat out reams of yellow paper. The old hands treated them like museum pieces. They never quite trusted the room full of pampered computers just next door. Real paper and ink-stained fingers; a reporter should sweat, they said. That was the way things were accomplished before tape drive memories and a CRT screen at every desk. Nancy sensed that most of it was fluff, but she enjoyed the old stories. They were a part of her profession and she was proud of its folklore and past.

Nancy's walk quickened, as though to keep pace with the energy level around her. Daily tragedy and disaster, crammed in between commercials, paid two hundred salaries and kept the city watching twice a night. She continued down a long corridor of metal desks, past the news writers and editorial staff, toward the hot white television lights at the far end of the floor.

"Nancy!"

She stopped and turned around. Marsha Ward waved frantically to her from the entrance of her cubicle. Suddenly Nancy remembered the interview. She felt her face begin to flush. Her associate producer hurried toward her.

"Nancy, I've been trying to get you for hours. Where have you been?" Marsha's voice carried more concern than anger.

"I'm sorry I'm late. There's still plenty of time."

"No there isn't. We're going to need the piece on Guru Mashtavani live. The deputy mayor finked out, and . . ." Marsha's voice dropped off to a whisper. She peered over the tops of her heavy glasses until her eyes caught Nancy's and held her fast. "Nan, you look tired. Is anything wrong?"

"Of course not," Nancy answered defensively.

"If you say so," Marsha conceded. That matter settled, her tone turned crisply efficient. "I dropped the Guru's bio off on your desk. He's in makeup now, trying to capture the alpha state. He still thinks the interview is going to be taped. I won't tell him it's live until the last minute."

Nancy found herself barely listening.

"Can I talk to you later, Marsha? It's personal."

"You can talk to me right now." Marsha beckoned her back toward the cubicle. Nancy took two steps to follow, then stopped. The speech she had composed stuck in her throat.

"No, not now, please. After the broadcast. I've really got to prep for the interview." She knew it was a passable excuse, but she could not meet Marsha's eyes. *Does she know?* Nancy wondered as she walked nervously to her own desk.

The yellow phone messages were neatly stacked atop the manila folder in the center of her desk. She leafed through them quickly, hoping none would require a response. Two were from the same caller. She ignored the others. Her fingers fumbled with the dial. She tapped her foot impatiently as the phone rang, and rang.

"Regency Hotel."

"Mr. Addison, please. Room 1420." Be there, she whispered. The line clicked to hold and the connection was made.

"Yes?" A man answered on the first ring. The sound of his voice brought Nancy an elating wave of relief.

"Bill, I just got your message. What are you doing in New York? God, I feel so miserable. You're the only person I want to see. I've just got to talk to you." She exhaled in one long breath.

"Nan, slow down." Addison was shocked by the compelling urgency of her voice. "What's wrong?"

Nancy stopped herself just short of telling him. There was too much to it. "Bill, I've got to see you. This has been the longest, the worst three weeks of my life."

"Of course. When are you free? You know you're the only reason I've come to New York."

Nancy mentally ran down her schedule. "I'll be finished here by seven. Can you meet me at the English Grill?"

"The place where we watched the ice skaters?"

"Yes. By the way, how was Tokyo?"

"Expensive. Dreary. I'll tell you about it when I see you. In the meantime, just relax. And don't forget I love you."

William Addison was smiling as he put down the receiver. She's finally done it, or at least decided to do it, he thought. She's told John about us. He's going to give her a divorce. He'll be a bastard about it, but in the end, what else can he do? The more he considered it, the more firmly the idea took hold. In a moment, the stale aftertaste of his long flight had vanished. His mind raced ahead to the details of their new lives. Would Nancy be willing to take a job in Washington? Perhaps he should think about buying a larger house. And cutting down on all that travel. Only the sight of his battered canvas suitcase propped against the bed brought him back to reality. The international security business could hardly be run by phone. The problems he had to solve were whispered behind closed doors. To hell with it, he decided in a burst of optimism. Whatever it is, we'll work it out together.

Addison slid the photograph out of his wallet and held it close to the bed lamp. It was the only one he had of them together. He even recalled the stranger who had taken it for them on the quiet beach. The contrast was striking. Nancy appeared singularly fair and fragile standing beside his leathery sun-darkened body. The sight of her reminded him to take the parcel out of his briefcase. He set it on the dressing table beside the photograph, where he would be sure to see it before he left. Not that he would have really forgotten it. He had gone on a three-thousand-mile detour to buy it for Nancy.

Technicians yawned behind the control-room glass. Nancy wished the interview would finally end, or the studio lights would mercifully blow out. She had done her best but had no doubt that Marsha would not schedule another guru for a long time to come. The Guru finally ended his baleful chant and the camera cut away. Mitch, the director, drew a finger across his throat. Nancy smiled into the red light and signed off. She couldn't wait to get out of the studio.

Marsha caught up with her at the elevator. "I'd get out of town fast too, after an interview like that." Then she shrugged and tossed her scarf over her shoulder. "So the Guru thought he could sing. Forget it. Let's go for a drink. You can tell old Marsha what's been bugging you the last couple of weeks."

"Tomorrow. I promise, Marsha. There's somebody I have to tell first."

"Okay, but Matt and I are worried about you."

"I know. Thanks. You've been a good friend."

Marsha backed off a step. For a moment she reminded Nancy of herself when she was puzzled or upset.

"You make it sound so . . . so final."

Nancy turned her head just as the elevator door opened. Marsha never saw the tears glistening in her eyes.

Addison arrived at Rockefeller Center fifteen minutes early. His walk had been as brisk as the cold December air. Fifth Avenue was dressed for Christmas, but he hardly noticed. He realized it had been that way for the past year. Whenever he thought of Nancy, there was little room for anything else. He paused at the top of the steps to watch the ice skaters glide across the world's most valuable rink. It lay like a white carpet in front of the RCA Building. Just behind it the six-story Christmas tree glittered with brightly colored lights against the semidarkness. For all his visits, Addison retained his tourist's eye. New York was the place people came to have fun.

He identified the Grill by its long gracefully curved window, contoured to the oval shape of the rink. Every table had a view. Nancy had invited him to lunch there on the day they met. It had taken three phone calls, but he finally consented to be interviewed.

At first they talked about his profession, how antiterrorist security worked. She probed him for an angle. Who were the victims? How could they be taught to protect themselves? What sort of person would declare himself a murderer and an enemy of society? Her questions came like a barrage of sharp left jabs. Nancy had done her homework. Addison recalled his first sloppy answer. Nancy's lips had curled into a frown and she began to drum the table lightly with her fingertips like an impatient schoolteacher. Addison threw up his hands and broke into a respectful grin.

"Lady," he said, "you know how to pin a man's ears back."

He knew he was hooked.

Then she reviewed the questions she would ask on the air. They would talk about concepts and methods, but not his specific clients or his specific targets. He would have talked about anything she wanted. They had not been back since, but he would not dream of going to the skating rink with anyone else.

Addison maneuvered past the crowd at the bar, toward the tables near the window where he could watch the skaters while he waited. The maître d' smiled professionally as Addison approached.

"How many in your party, sir?"

"Bill!"

Addison picked the chime of her voice out of the racket of noisy drinkers. Then he saw Nancy rise from her table. The next moment he felt her arms tightly around his shoulders. The crowd vanished. All his senses drank her in. She was light in his arms and responded like a dancer to his touch. He squeezed her tightly.

"Nan, I can't believe it's been almost a month. I've missed you more then I thought I could."

She stiffened slightly, drawing back as though suddenly embarrassed that they were embracing in a public place.

Addison held her at arm's length to look into her eyes a moment longer. One day he would admit that the austere tweed business suits she favored had the perverse effect of heightening his desire to caress her lithe body.

"Bill, sometimes I thought you were never coming back."

"You're too beautiful for that. You look . . ."

"Thinner." The smile faded quietly from Nancy's lips as she led the way back to her table. A waiter appeared almost immediately with two drinks. Nancy anticipated Addison's question.

"I ordered them. You're so punctual. Cheers."

The toast sounded cold and flat to Addison's ears.

"Is that all you can say to the man you love? 'Cheers'?" he asked lightly.

"I'm sorry."

There was a melancholy distance in her voice that Addison had never heard before. He thrust out the parcel, hoping it would change her mood.

"I brought you back a little something from the exotic Orient. Go ahead. Open it."

Nancy reached across the table. Her restraint gradually gave way to excitement as she undid the knot.

"I hope you didn't go to any trouble. . . . Bill, my God, it's beautiful." She lifted the jade necklace out of its cotton wadding and held it in front of her. Light sparkled off the faceted stones as they swayed delicately with the movement of her hands. "I can't accept this," she said at last.

"Why not?"

"It must be worth a fortune. I can't. Not now."

"Consider it a large engagement ring."

Nancy set the necklace gently back in its wrapping.

"I can't do that, either."

Addison leaned forward across the small table. "I thought you and I . . ."

There was no need for him to say any more. The glow in his eyes told Nancy all she had to know. For a moment she was angry, as though his desires had leaped to the center of her stage to steal her grand scene. The feeling faded as quickly as it came, replaced by the warm glow of pleasant memories. She found the prospect of putting her problems aside for an hour very appealing. Her fingers stroked the back of his hand. She had already made up her mind.

"Back to the Regency?" she said quietly, enjoying the smile that spread across his face.

The suite was as familiar as her own apartment. Nancy tossed her coat over the back of a gaily upholstered Queen Anne chair. Her shoes went skittering across the carpet, right to the edge of the bed. Her knees trembled with excitement. She could barely wait for Addison to wrap his arms around her. She wanted to be held tightly. To shut out the rest of the world. In a moment his strong fingers began to loosen the tight muscles of her back and thighs. She felt herself melting against him. Her hands slowly traced their way down his sides. Whatever you've got, Nancy thought in a rare moment of happiness, nobody ever said it was contagious.

The light was a sliver of gray between the heavy drapes. Nancy knew the fantasy was over. She looked at Addison. He was wide-awake, staring at the ceiling. He turned to her and smiled as his hand clasped hers tightly. Tell him quickly, she thought, or you'll never do it at all.

"Bill, something happened while you were gone. Everything's changed . . . I . . . I've changed. Or been changed."

"What is it, darling?" Addison asked.

"I'm sick, Bill." She had practiced the phrase many times. Now it sounded like someone else's voice echoing down a long tunnel. "They tell me I'm going to die . . . in a few weeks. Of something called military fever."

Addison felt the chill that ran through Nancy's body. He had trained himself to watch people's eyes when they spoke, and the little things they did with their hands. Nancy's hands were folded across her chest. All that was missing was a lily clasped between her fingers. His instincts told him she was serious. Yet his mind had a will of its own.

"You must be joking." You fool, he thought instantly.

Nancy's eyes began to moisten. "Nancy, military what? It sounds like some damned trench mouth. How do you know?"

"Bill, I'm not some dumb bimbo. I know. Isn't that enough for you? It's been checked and rechecked. The disease is also called Percy's fever. You like that name better? Dr. Francis Percy wrote the first treatise in 1415. He called it pernicious vapors. English survivors of the battle of Agincourt were dropping like flies in their barracks in Calais. It worked something like the plague, only a lot slower. Now I'm told that Dr. Percy was all wet. It isn't caused by evil spirits or bad blood. Military fever is some damned obscure parasite that's host for an even more obscure strain of bacteria. The doctors are guessing that I picked it up last summer in India. Jesus, the last reported case in America was in 1947. They just don't know what the hell to do." She choked back the sob rising in her throat. She hated what she was about to say. "Bill, I can't see you again. I guess it's over . . . like my life."

Nancy slowly got out of bed and began gathering up her clothes. Addison watched her in stunned amazement. Then he jumped up beside her. His hand shot out, grabbing her around the wrist. He stood so close that he could feel her heart pounding and see his face in her watery eyes.

"I love you," he whispered. "There must be something we can do. We're not just going to accept it."

Nancy felt the fear and anger drain out of her body. What was left was a feeling of weakness and fatigue. She leaned forward until her head was resting against his shoulder. Then she let him guide her back to bed. She knew it wouldn't change anything.

"Please understand, Bill. I want to be with you, but sometimes love isn't enough. I can't leave John now. God, what a pathetic sight he was. He cried like a baby when he found out. Really. I didn't think he was capable of tears. If I left him now, he'd despise himself forever. Besides, it wouldn't be fair to you. We'd have no more then a few weeks together. Believe me, I've thought this out from the first moment I knew. It's best this way."

"No!" Addison exhaled the word like a cry of pain. "There's still a chance. There must be."

But this time he didn't try to stop her when she got up. She turned when she reached the doorway. For an instant she wanted to run back, quickly before he disappeared from her life. But instead she turned her eyes to the brightly lit corridor. A sudden gust of wind blew the door shut behind her.

2

Dr. Amos Stepp brushed aside the huge stack of reports that cluttered the coffee table in front of him. When he looked up, his dark eyes were sparkling under the bushy gray brows that somehow accentuated his total baldness.

"It's time for plain speaking, Arch," he said to the younger man who watched him from behind a massive mahogany desk. "If we don't go with Nancy Seymour we might as well scrap the whole project. She's the perfect candidate. We could search for fifty years without finding another quite like her."

Arch Kholer shook his head. As chairman of North American Chemicals, the final decision was his alone. He turned to the third man in the office. "You've heard him, George. Now the ball's in your court." Kholer's fingers drummed out a staccato march tempo as he spoke. Lawyers bored him. "Is the procedure legal?" His voice became sharp. "Just keep it to a simple yes or no."

George Snead leaned forward until his elbows almost touched Kholer's desk. His red face was a masque of thought. He hated to put his firm's reputation on the line without one shred of precedent. But North American Chemicals was his most lucrative client. Kholer turned away from him to watch the view of New York harbor forty floors below. The few seconds of respite did not help Snead. He fought simple answers the way a gardener battles weeds.

"Well?" Kholer snapped. "Dr. Stepp and I have to get on with it. Can NAC perform this cryonic procedure without getting sued right into bankruptcy court?"

Kholer's going to snap this up, no matter what George Snead says, Stepp thought. No lawyer is going to talk him out of it. He's too greedy.

"I suppose so," Snead answered in a whisper. "Right now, based on information we have in hand . . ."

Stepp smiled with satisfaction. As he anticipated, Snead immediately began to itemize all sorts of qualifications.

"The patient must be legally dead," Snead pointed out. "That's absolutely essential before you can begin the cryonic process. You'll want witnesses. Then I suppose if she has willed her body to science, you can go ahead with any sort of experiment."

"Experiment, Snead." Stepp was on his feet advancing toward the lawyer. "Don't be so damned patronizing. Nancy Seymour has got military fever. It's been certified by the Center for Disease Control in Atlanta. She's walking around dead right now. How can we possibly hurt her?"

"That is not the issue, Doctor."

"Mr. Snead, it is very important to Mr. Kholer and myself that we get a clean legal opinion." Stepp spoke slowly, as though addressing a backward pupil. "We don't want any stockholder suits, class actions, estate suits, or any of the legal nightmares that drive people out of windows. Her husband works for us. He's signed every release you've stuck under his nose. The only consideration he required is that we diligently seek a cure. We are doing so, to the tune of a substantial expenditure. Nancy signed the will you prepared. So much for the estate argument. Preceding the cryonic procedure, Nancy Seymour will be certified stone-cold dead by the Mayo Brothers and the pope if you like. Then we freeze her. If and when we find a cure for military fever, we thaw her out. Maybe she survives, maybe not. No guarantees. Snead, what the devil could be perfectly simpler? Now, all I require is your learned written opinion that it is also perfectly legal."

Snead looked down at the floor. "I find the whole concept distasteful. Think of what you are proposing, Doctor. You want to raise the dead. How can I certify an action I consider ludicrous and basically wrong?"

"Enough of this bickering, both of you," Kholer cut them off sharply. Then the hard, scowling lines around his mouth gave way to a smile and he looked years younger. "George, I admit I was also skeptical at first. Our research people have been tinkering with this cryonics business for years. We've had some success with organs—livers, kidneys, and such—but a whole damned person . . . Come on, George, that's exciting. We're giving life. What could be so wrong with that? North American Chemicals will be the first to bring a human being back from the dead."

"Only a *legal* death." Stepp wagged his finger as he began to pace the length of the large office. "Cryonic suspension is not death, Arch. Is a toaster dead when you pull out the plug? The body mechanism simply ceases to function for the time being. As long as the organs are protected against decomposition, a body could be suspended forever. We're fortunate, indeed, to have found the perfect subject."

Snead got to his feet. He had heard all he needed to make his decision. He knew he was walking on the thin edge of looking for a new client. Ultimately, he thought, Kholer is right. Business is business.

"Go ahead with it," he said. "I'll provide you with a written opinion that your insurance companies should be able to swallow. I'm sure you gentlemen know what is best for NAC."

Stepp watched Snead leave and immediately began to pack his own papers. He had clearly won his point and saw no reason to risk overselling. Kholer's voice stopped him in his tracks.

"Have you seen her, Amos?" Kholer asked wistfully. He had opened one of the folders and was smiling at a photo of Nancy Seymour. "She's really very beautiful. I think it is a wonderful thing that NAC might be able to save her. That goes beyond the money. But tell me honestly, do you really think there is a chance we can bring her back?"

"It's possible." Stepp shrugged coldly. "As you've seen in my report, the monkey almost survived."

3

The key was clumsy in Nancy's hand as she fumbled to fit it into the lock. She knew the hallway light was no worse than usual, and it was the same lock she had opened a thousand times without difficulty. She squinted hard and tried to concentrate as she fought back the urge to curse out loud. Then she felt the cold wave of fear. It was a feeling that had lurked just below the surface for the past three weeks. Bundy had warned her. Coordination would become difficult. She swung her fist in rage just as the door popped open.

"Nancy, I thought I heard something." Dr. John Victor's angular face was lined with worry as he reached out to take her arm. He led her slowly across the foyer and down the two steps into their living room. He could feel her muscles quivering as he helped her off with her coat.

"Where have you been? It's almost midnight. You should have been home from the studio hours ago." Then he shook his head from side to side like an exasperated parent. "Well, what did your Dr. Bundy have to say?"

Nancy sank down on the sofa. All she could think about was getting to sleep. But Victor stood over her, thumbs tucked into the pockets of his vest. Gradually he leaned forward until she could see the lines of worry etched in his

13

youthful face. At least he cares, she thought. For a moment she wondered if he knew about Addison, too. It wouldn't have surprised her a bit.

"He said I have to make up my own mind. He doesn't know enough about cryonics to even evaluate NAC's test results." She thought she heard Victor breathe out a low sigh of relief, but when she looked up, he was gone.

She found herself reaching for one of the news magazines neatly fanned out across the coffee table. The stack was almost too precise to disturb. She knew, without bothering to look, that the rest of their large apartment was equally tidy. A faint smile crossed her face as she recalled the better days of their marriage. Then she would tell John that he would make some girl a wonderful wife. No dirty dishes or piles of clothing, and dust wouldn't last an hour under his finicky eye. Before her illness, his half of the apartment looked like an operating room compared to hers. Now he cleaned the entire house and she had to admit that it had never looked so spotless.

"Time for your medicine." Victor sounded almost cheerful. His blue eyes sparkled as he placed the tray down in front of Nancy. Two red and one green pill were set on a silver dish, to be washed down with a large glass of warm milk. She hated the milk, but Victor insisted, and it had become a nightly ritual. In spite of herself, she had to admit that it helped her sleep.

"When you finish your milk, I've drawn a nice warm bath for you."

"John, I really wish you wouldn't fuss over me. It makes me feel so guilty. My God, before this happened, we hadn't even been speaking. Now you're acting like my doctor—and my mother."

"Don't be ridiculous. This thing is bigger than our personal problems. I *am* your doctor, along with others, and I'm going to do my damnedest to cure you. Then, if you still want a divorce . . ." He shrugged, but she could see the pain in his eyes. Sometimes, lately, she had to think hard to recall all the traits she had disliked in her husband. She admitted that he hadn't taken a drink or gambled a dollar in the weeks since Dr. Bundy had told him of her illness. It was what he had promised, and he had kept his word. Even in the dim light, Nancy could see that it had done him good. The puffiness around his eyes had receded and his wavy blond hair made him appear far younger then his forty-five years.

"John, I've been thinking about the cryonic suspension . . ."

"Don't feel that you have to make a decision right away. Remember, Dr. Stepp told you that you still have a week to think it over. Use the time."

He can be so reasonable, she thought. Even the milk didn't taste too bad. Suddenly she realized she was gripping the glass with both hands to keep it steady. Victor exhaled a long, sad breath.

"You know, you've got to do something about notifying the station. You can't keep working in your condition. It's not fair to you or to them."

He had hit a sore nerve. "You're right. It really isn't fair to them," Nancy answered after a long, thoughtful pause. "I can't put it off any longer. But they don't have to know the whole story. I don't think I could stand their pity. I'll apply for a medical leave of absence. I can be vague about the reasons."

Victor laid his hand lightly on the back of her neck. Then he rubbed it in a way she used to enjoy, long ago, in the good days of their courtship.

"I know how much you love your work. Just be sure to tell them to hold on to your job. You'll be back."

4

Executive producer Matt Sharp had the only office in the newsroom. It was a glass-walled cubicle at the center of the floor. When he opened his drapes he could look out on three sides. Sometimes he would stand at one of the windows, like a ship's captain on his bridge, and that usually meant something was wrong. Nancy could see him from the moment she left the elevator. He looked just the same as he had seven years before, on her first day at NBC. Then he had seemed stern and unapproachable; he was the only man on the job she referred to as Mr., even when she was talking to others about him. She had been wrong, and it taught her something about first impressions.

Suddenly Nancy realized how quiet it was. The machines were running, but something was missing. She looked quickly down the rows of linoleum, desks stacked with papers and coffee cups. Nobody was talking. The aisles were clear. There was no cluster of bodies to block her view of the water cooler. No games when Matt's watching, she thought with a smile. But it faded just as quickly. For a moment she wanted to walk back to her desk and forget the appointment. She could see the bright lights of the studio at the end of the floor. The production crew was checking the props and mikes

16

and camera angles for the night's broadcast. Don't change a thing, she thought fervently. I'll be back. Then Matt Sharp opened his door.

"Got tired of waiting for you to knock, Nancy," he said with loud good humor. It was a tone he rarely used, and it made Nancy even more uncomfortable.

"Well, aren't you going to come inside?"

Marsha Ward got up from her chair beside Sharp's desk and joined Nancy on the small sofa. Sharp walked around the office snapping shut the drapes. Nancy's stomach tightened as she watched him. The small office had always smelled like an old car on a hot day. Sharp's cigar smoke coated the walls with a fine film of greasy resins. But now it smelled almost . . . good, she thought. There wasn't a cigar in sight. They know, Nancy thought in a flash. Somebody told them.

"Matt, Marsha, it isn't what you think. Really. I just need some time off. A medical leave for a few months."

Sharp returned to his desk and started shuffling a stack of papers.

"What do I think?" he asked innocently. His trace of a smile had faded and Nancy searched his broad face for a clue.

"All I know," Sharp continued, "is that I've got this letter from your doctor . . . Dr. Bundy, and a confirmation from our own medical department. They agree that you need a rest. Company policy says you're entitled. I'll be sorry to lose you, Nancy, even for a couple of months."

"I'm sorry to be leaving." Nancy wanted to say more, but she could feel the lump rising in her throat. Marsha reached over and squeezed her hand.

"We've made it effective immediately, for as long as you need," she said in a whisper. "But the job's yours whenever you want it back. Just give me a call and I'll have you on the air the next day. Right, Matt?"

"You bet."

"Thank you both." Nancy could feel her self-control beginning to slip away. She bit her lip hard to keep back her tears. Now it was just a question of picking up her things and leaving as quickly and quietly as possible. It's a good thing you cleared your desk last night, she thought. She would telephone her friends later. She knew they would understand.

She fixed her eyes on her own desk and walked directly

toward it. It was at the rear of a row of six, just in front of the noisiest bank of teletype machines. Today it was the only one with a perfectly empty surface. That's the way it is when somebody leaves or gets fired, she thought. It happens often enough. She hoped no one would pay any attention to her.

She walked briskly, intent on the cardboard box that sat beside her chair. It was filled with tokens and memories that made it very precious. In spite of herself, she began rechecking the drawers, opening and closing them as unobtrusively as she could. She looked up, aware that something wasn't quite right. The background-noise level had dropped to practically nothing. Then she saw the people who had converged from all over the floor. Her friends. She looked from one bleak face to the next, wondering frantically what she could say. No one advanced. They just stood silently, watching her, as though as invisible barrier prevented them from intruding. Then the crowd parted and Matt Sharp burst through.

"You didn't think we'd let you sneak out without a big hug." His booming voice broke the spell. He wrapped his arms around Nancy's waist and lifted her off the ground. The others joined in and she felt their warm embraces from all sides. Her composure dissolved in a wash of tears as friends kissed her and pumped her hand as if she had just won an election. Then Sharp took hold of her arm and guided her toward the elevator.

"Don't worry," he whispered in her ear. "We all love you."

5

Nancy didn't want to open her eyes. She rolled over on her side, but she could still feel the sunlight streaming in through her bedroom window. She lay still a moment longer, gathering her strength to fight back the lingering effects of the sleeping pills. They weighed her down like lead and she hated having to take them. It was a running battle between sleep and fear. Sometimes she almost preferred the fear.

She gritted her teeth and sat upright. It was an act of resistance more than necessity. There was no place she had to be that morning. Not until the afternoon, she remembered, when Victor gets back. Then there would be more forms and papers and legal documents. Dying's so damned much work, she thought. Why doesn't everybody just forget about it? The ring of the telephone startled her. She shook the last cobwebs out of her mind and lifted the receiver.

"Nancy, I tried the studio. Are you alone? I have to talk to you."

"Yes, Bill, I'm alone," she answered coldly.

"I couldn't leave New York without talking to you, if only to let you know that I respect your feelings. Who knows, maybe you're right. So I won't be calling again, since you insist. But I want you to know that I won't stop thinking about you, and I won't stop loving you."

Nancy wanted to respond to the warmth in his voice, as she had so many times before. But she knew that would only make everything more difficult.

"That means a great deal to me, Bill. But I honestly think my decision is for the best. Good-bye . . . and thank you." She hung up. Tears were running down her cheeks. She felt a great emptiness.

Pull yourself together, she told herself. Things are going to get a lot worse before they get better. You said they'd have to drag you off kicking and screaming. Start acting like it. That had been Owen Bundy's advice, and he was the wisest person she knew. For a moment she wanted to pick up the phone and call him, but she stopped herself. Bundy was a first-rate doctor, but he was still only a doctor. He had done everything he could. She could still see the pained look on his round, cherubic face as he read the report of her NBC physical only a few weeks ago.

"There's no doubt now, Nancy," he had said with his usual honesty. "Our diagnosis was confirmed by the Center for Disease Control. It's military fever. They're guessing that you picked it up from the water while you were in India last summer. It could have been a drop on a leaf of lettuce, or the ice cube in a drink. The disease is so rare that it's remarkable your company doctor was able to diagnose it correctly. Just chance that he'd spent time in Asia and knew something about these swamp fevers." Bundy studied Nancy's face to judge how much more he could tell her. He knew what was coming.

"What is it?" Nancy tried to keep her voice from cracking.

"It's a virulent bacterial growth that appears to be carried in polluted water, sewage, and the like, much like typhus. The first cases were reported in Europe as long as five hundred years ago. In its last stages it resembles the bubonic plague. That part fooled the doctors for quite some time. It has a cancerlike resistance to antibiotics." Bundy paused. "Nancy, you should know that it is almost always fatal. Do you want me to tell you what little more we've uncovered?"

Nancy nodded her head, and Bundy resumed. "As recently as the 1890's there were still hundreds of cases being reported. Then it seemed to disappear. Diseases do that sometimes for absolutely no reason we can figure out. We still get an occasional reported case, but almost always from the tropics. We haven't had one in the United States for thirty-five years."

"Isn't there a cure for it?" Nancy asked.

"Since there are so few cases, nobody has bothered working on a specific cure. Research money goes for the big problems. Now that we have the technology, I'm reasonably certain it could be done . . . but we'd have to start from scratch. Your blood cultures seem to indicate that some kind of antibody might be effective in mustering your body's natural defenses. But, Nancy, isolating that antibody is still strictly trial and error. Computers will speed the process. Still, it could take months, or longer. And it would cost a fortune."

Nancy could only stare at her physician. At last she spoke. "How long have I got?"

Bundy shook his head. "It's impossible to say precisely. We've already begun to observe what we believe are some of the terminal symptoms. The pain in your joints, intermittent drowsiness, loss of coordination and muscle tone. It's all part of the syndrome. We can give you drugs for the symptoms. You shouldn't be too uncomfortable. . . ."

"How long, Owen?" Nancy pressed.

"Four, maybe five weeks."

That was two weeks ago. Since then Nancy had conjured with her grim but remotely hopeful alternative—to submit to cryonic suspension: to be frozen in a kind of living death until a cure for her disease could be developed.

Nancy shook her head as if to clear it. All at once she knew what she had to do. Her hands shook as she punched out the number of her garage.

"Charlie, this is Nancy Seymour. Can you have my car out front in half an hour?"

It's got to be today, she told herself, while you can still function and make up your own mind. The pain in her shoulders came creeping back like a sharp spur. Not severe enough to make her scream, just a stern reminder that her time was slipping by. She knew she would have to take a painkiller eventually. It had become a game to see how long she could hold out. The intervals were growing shorter.

Nancy recalled how Victor had made the drive up to NAC in little over an hour. The Porsche had flowed through traffic without a jerk or swerve. But for her it was pure torture. The car jumped and whined like a mean-spirited animal. She crept along in the right lane as the cars shot past, horns blasting. She ignored them and gradually began to feel some confidence. There was never a question of turning back. If she was going to submit to cryonic suspension, the sooner the better. But she had to see the tank before she could make her decision.

6

The sprawling glass-and-concrete building covered an entire hilltop just above the parking lot. Nancy stared up at it as though she were preparing to scale a great mountain. She judged the number of steps and the pitch of the path leading to the prominent double doors. She knew it was nothing, a short suburban walk from the car to the office. The thought made her angry with herself. She shoved open the car door and stepped gingerly into the cold afternoon air. A burst of pain knifed through her stomach. She leaned over the hood, feeling cold metal through her coat.

"You all right, miss?"

The voice took her by surprise. She turned to see a red-faced security guard standing a few feet away, watching her carefully. He probably thinks I'm drunk, she thought. The pain had eased a bit. She wanted to speak clearly.

"Yes, of course." Suddenly the walk to the front door seemed like an impossible task. She could see no point in lying. "No. I'm ill."

The guard looked her over warily.

"I'm here to see Dr. Stepp," she added quickly. For a moment she expected him to click his heels together.

"Yes, ma'am. May I help you? I can have a wheelchair brought down."

"No. That's all right."

But he offered Nancy his arm and she took it.

"You're Miss Seymour, aren't you? My whole family watches your show," he said softly, more to comfort her than give information. "You just hang on. I'll have you inside in a jiffy."

Nancy looked up at the puffy red, smiling face. The man was old enough to be her father. You should be helping him, she thought miserably.

"You're very kind," she said, trying to bear as much of her own weight as she could. "What's your name?"

"Frank, ma'am. Just call me Frank."

Ma'am. The word went off like an alarm bell in her brain. You must really look terrific when a sixty-five-year-old calls you "ma'am," she thought.

The reception area seemed as large as the parking lot. Frank led Nancy to the nearest sofa. Then he started off at a trot toward the raised slab of granite that served as a reception desk. "North American Chemicals" was spelled out in three-foot-high letters across the wall behind it. Nancy glanced at the product display cases and the men with bulky briefcases who also waited. She saw Frank whisper something to the young receptionist. She jumped to her feet as though her chair were on fire. A moment later she was smiling down at Nancy.

"Miss Seymour, Dr. Stepp told us to expect you. But we didn't know exactly when. I'm afraid the doctor's in conference at the moment. If there's anything I can do . . ."

Please don't call me "ma'am," Nancy thought. "I've really come to see the cryonics division. Dr. Stepp told me I could visit anytime."

"Yes, of course. Frank can escort you."

"I'd prefer to go alone."

The receptionist knit her brow.

"I'm feeling much better," Nancy added.

"If you're sure." She handed Nancy a large plastic badge marked "Special Guest—NAC." "It's on the fourth floor. I'll alert all stations."

Nancy's hand was halfway into her purse before the elevator door slid shut. She feared her knees would buckle before she could wrench open her child proof pill bottle. She swallowed two in one gulp. In a moment the pain in her back and legs began to fade. She had bought about an hour of peace. A week before, two pills would have held her for an entire day. Watch out or you'll become a Demerol junkie, she thought ruefully, if you live long enough.

The elevator opened on a small platform enclosed by a glass wall. A guard sat behind a desk on the other side. Beyond him Nancy could see corridors of offices and people in white coats walking purposefully between them.

"Miss Seymour?" The guard's voice sounded tinny through the intercom.

"Yes."

"Please inset your badge in the slot." He motioned to a small box mounted on the door frame. It was a security device Nancy had seen on bank vaults and military installations. The guard snapped to attention as the door opened. A red light blinked on his console.

"Our metal detector," he explained. "Would you try again, without your purse, please."

Nancy set her purse on his desk and stepped back through the open doorway. This time there was no light.

"Even car keys'll set it off," he said pleasantly. "We've got to be pretty careful. You can empty it out, or leave it with me if you like. That's what most people do."

Nancy thought about her pills. She hoped she wouldn't need them.

"I'm here to see the laboratory."

"That's the east wing, Miss Seymour. Do you know how to operate one of these?" He patted the arm of a small golf cart beside his desk.

"For me?" she asked with surprise.

"Naw, this place is so big that all our executives use them to get around. I just happen to have a spare. Go ahead and take it."

She knew he was lying, but it was a kindly lie that saved her pride. The golf cart, she suspected, was Dr. Stepp's idea. At that moment she was very grateful for his thoroughness. The corridor would, indeed, have been a long and painful walk. But the cart rolled quickly and silently over the highly polished floors. The walls were covered with brightly colored fabrics and the offices she passed were all small, moveable cubicles. There was none of the clatter she was used to at NBC. The people and machines hummed. The corridor abruptly ended at another glass wall. The notice over the card box read "Cryonics Research—Restricted Area—No Unauthorized Personnel." A battery of closed-circuit television cameras surrounded the door. The badge alone was not sufficient. The guard on the other side punched a code into his console. Then the door slid open. He waved Nancy into a waiting hospital-sized utility elevator.

Nancy was impressed. She sensed crisp efficiency, and a lot of money spent. That was important to her. Cryonics had to be respectable before she could take it seriously. She remembered Dr. Stepp sipping his Scotch and trying to sound casual the first time he raised the subject. For a moment she rekindled the sick, angry feeling that had boiled in her stomach. She had almost told Stepp to leave her home. But John had sensed her outrage and stepped between them like a referee at a fight.

"Please, Nancy, hear him out. He's made a special trip just to see you," he said. "Certainly it's gruesome, but so is dying of military fever. You're not a child. Amos simply wants you to have all the facts. Would you have it any other way?"

She knew he was right.

"I grant you, Nancy," Stepp had continued in his flat, monotone voice, "to date cryonics has languished in the suburbs of scientific recognition. And not without cause. The type and quality of people in the field would give a bad name to loan-sharking. But we're North American Chemicals. We do things right."

"I don't quite understand what you're offering me, Dr. Stepp," she said cautiously, trying to force the image of a gauze-swaddled mummy from her brain.

"A chance, nothing more," he answered. "You'll be contributing to science, but I doubt that's very important to you."

Nancy appreciated his candor. To Amos Stepp, her death was neither embarrassing nor painful. For the first time she found she could talk about it without watching her listener cringe.

"You're right. All I want to do is live."

"Very reasonable. Now, I ask you to approach cryonics with an open mind. Consider it another of the myriad of discoveries that have changed our lives over the past few decades. How many things that once seemed so fanciful are now everyday realities? Remember, my dear, our cryonics research was originally sponsored by NASA. That's your tax dollars. NASA is still convinced that we must place astronauts in stasis in order to make possible voyages into deep space. That ought to give us a whiff of credibility."

"Why have you selected me, Doctor? Is it because John works for NAC?"

"Heavens, no!" Stepp exclaimed emphatically. "You can lay your guilty conscience to rest on that score. If anything, it worked against you. We've got hundreds of applicants. People are dying to get into the program." He smiled at his pun. "This is our first—and perhaps only—shot. Everything has to be absolutely aboveboard. Frankly, the nepotism business worried me. But I chose you anyway because military fever is a disease we're sure we can cure, and in a relatively short time. That's the key, Nancy. We can't revive you until we can cure you. As long as we're being candid, there was another factor to be weighed. You'll die with minimal visible physical damage. This is America, my dear. People like pretty people."

Stepp's cold logic was as infuriating as it was refreshing. It's just the kind of treatment you said you wanted, Nancy thought. Now you've got it. She realized that her personal feelings about Stepp made no difference at all. To him, her death was a matter of business.

"What happens next, Doctor?" She wanted to sound equally businesslike.

"You think about what I've said. You'll be deteriorating rapidly, so the sooner you come to a decision, the better all around. That way we can keep you under close surveillance right up to the end. Get yourself mangled in a car accident or something like that, and you're out of the program. Our laboratory has a first-class medical-research facility; that's where we want you to die. That way cryonic immersion can begin immediately upon our certification of your death. We want to keep all your cells nice and fresh. Has John ever taken you up to our Fairfield laboratory?"

"Once, before he was transferred to the New York office."

"Well, then, you know the way. Come up anytime. I'd like to have you inspect the facility. Look around, kick some tires. Get rid of the notion that we're a pack of lunatic scientists puttering around in some castle dungeon."

The elevator stopped two floors down. Nancy eased her golf cart past a long bank of computers. The machines appeared to be running themselves. There was nobody in sight. Nancy glanced at her watch. It was almost five o'clock. Just as well, she decided. No one had ever been able to satisfactorily explain the workings of a computer to her. She lacked the mental energy to try again. The tidy little offices around the periphery of the computer room were also empty. She passed them quickly, heading toward the only corridor out. The soft lighting and carpeting made it far more inviting than the antiseptic room full of machines. But it was the large window at the far end that caught her eye. She could see nothing but white beyond the glass. The corridor widened into a small amphitheater. It was a gallery area. Through the window and twenty feet below she saw a gleaming white operating room. A solitary figure in a surgical gown sat facing a CRT display mounted in the far wall. She watched him for a moment. His finger ran down a long computer printout sheet.

"Yes, my dear, that is where we will prepare you for cryonic suspension," Amos Stepp whispered in Nancy's ear. Her instinct was to jump, but she managed to remain still. Stepp leaned over and pushed a button on the railing in front of the window.

"Past quitting time, Willie," he said into a hidden microphone. "Time to close up."

Nancy barely caught a glimpse of him before a steel shutter descended over the window. Then the amphitheater lights brightened to the level of the computer room. She knew by the twinkle in Stepp's dark eyes that he was enjoying the chance to show off his toy.

"Very impressive, isn't it" he said, spreading his pudgy arms wide apart. "It's one of the finest operating rooms in the country. You can take my word on it. But now, my dear, I'll show you what you've really come to see. Mind if I drive?"

He deftly maneuvered the golf cart back up the ramp and out to the corridor. The familiarity of his manner gave Nancy the feeling she had known him for a long time.

"Who designed this facility, Doctor?" she asked.

"I did. With specifications provided by NASA. We're quite serious about cryonics."

He flipped a switch on the golf cart and a panel in the corridor wall slid up. They proceeded down a narrow ramp; out to a level, tiled floor. Then Nancy saw the smoke, It billowed up like an angry storm cloud a yard off the ground, covering the entire area of the glassed-in room in front of them. At the rear of the room she could see the upper portion of a large cylinder. Its lid was open. She immediately thought of a coffin.

"That's the tank, isn't it?" She pointed through the glass.

"You don't let anything distract you," Stepp said with a broad grin. "That's good. I like straight thinking. Yes, that will be your home while you're waiting peacefully for a cure. Don't mind the mist. It's only liquid nitrogen. The tank operates at a temperature approaching zero degrees Kelvin. We'll use contact lenses to protect your eyes. Your skin will be constantly bathed in a protective DMSO solution recycled through the tank. If it works as expected, you'll emerge without so much as a rash. That's important too."

"Will you keep the tank like that—open, I mean—while I'm . . . ?"

"Certainly not. You'd suffer irreparable tissue damage. That would undo all our prophylactic measures. My God, even the Egyptians knew enough to seal their tombs. But you will be seen through the plexiglass lid. No floor show, mind you. The worst possible thing we could do is cause a lot of hoopla and then not be able to bring you back. Can you imagine the embarrassment to NAC?"

"Not to mention my embarrassment."

"Yes, that too. But we will have appropriate members of the scientific community as observers. And doctors too. That wouldn't bother you, would it?"

"You make it sound like I've already given my consent, Dr. Stepp."

"Did I really?" Stepp asked casually. He turned Nancy's face to the light and looked her over with a cold, clinical gaze. Then he took her hand. His strong fingers massaged her knuckles while he took her pulse. "I've done quite a bit of reading on military fever recently, what bits and pieces are to be had. You must realize that you are well along. Without narcotic support, you would be bedridden and screaming right now."

Nancy knew he was right. "Have you made any progress on finding a cure?"

"Not yet," he answered sadly. "But we will, that much I promise. We've the money and the talent, and most important, Nancy, we have the commitment. It just takes time to isolate a virus. Trial and error. Even today, with all we know, science is still stuck with trial and error."

He sounded so despondent that Nancy wanted to laugh. She could almost picture him scurrying from one microscope to the next, like a chess master playing two dozen games at once. She found herself feeling a spark of warmth for the pudgy little man.

"I'll need a few more days to make up my mind, Doctor. Will that be all right?"

"Of course. Now, if you've seen enough, I'll have a car take you home. You really shouldn't be driving in your condition. We don't want to take any unnecessary risks, do we?"

Nancy lay perfectly still for a full half-hour before she would trust herself to speak. The drugs had made her dizzy, and almost nauseous. Finally, when she could wait no longer, she rolled over in bed and lifted the telephone. She had often used the private twenty-four-hour line and knew the number by heart.

"NBC News, Archives," a tired voice answered.

"This is Nancy Seymour," she said as crisply as she could manage. "I've got a rush job. I want everything you've got on a Dr. Amos Stepp. Have a messenger deliver the material to my home by ten tomorrow morning."

7

"Stepp's a damned genius, Owen. He's got a list of degrees and awards as long as your arm. He ran NASA's space-medicine program for three years before going over to NAC." Nancy's voice sank to a whisper. "You read his file. It would make more sense to you anyway. The guy is good. I'm convinced of it." She gritted her teeth and shifted her weight slightly on the hard chesterfield sofa. Dr. Owen Bundy watched her pain. He could almost feel it himself. He wanted to be tougher, but it just wasn't his nature.

"I guess," Bundy answered, as though he had barely heard Nancy's discourse on the career of Dr. Amos Stepp. It had been clear to him from the beginning which way she was leaning. "You want to go ahead with the cryonic suspension, don't you?"

"No!" Nancy answered emphatically. "Owen, do you know what they do to you? Stepp gave me all the technical jargon. But what it comes down to is that they drain out all your blood and pump you full of antifreeze. Then they store you in a tank full of liquid nitrogen. It's like being a zombie. You're dead, but you're not. Who the devil would want something like that?"

The outburst had exhausted her. She slumped back on the

31

sofa, letting her eyes wander over the rows of diplomas on the wall behind Bundy's desk. The rest of his large, softly lit office was lined, floor to ceiling, with bookshelves overflowing with leather-bound medical texts. She remembered that they had always looked dusty with disuse. But that was before her illness. Her face softened and she felt tears welling up behind her eyes. Bundy had worked so hard, and accomplished so little. It didn't matter. She loved him anyway, as she had loved her father while he was alive. They were friends in Omaha. When she came to New York, Owen Bundy was the first person she called. The fifteen years seemed like a lifetime ago.

"Owen, I want you to talk me out of it. I want you to tell me there's another way."

Bundy shook his head. He moved slowly from behind his desk to a chair facing Nancy. He's aged, she thought, as though the disease was spreading through him too. His hair had turned completely white, and his thin body grew more stooped and tired by the day.

"Nancy, you're entitled to a decent, dignified burial. That's everyone's right. I'm sure Dr. Stepp's done all the fine things your station's dug up on him. That doesn't mean he can bring a body back from the dead. Nobody can do that. Maybe I'm old-fashioned, but I'm glad that's the way it is. I know you're not very religious, Nancy, neither was your daddy. The way I see it, when you die, you're going home to God. No man can change that."

Why not? she wanted to shout. We've changed all the other rules.

"Stepp never promised it would work. He said it's a chance. Whatever happens, NAC will develop a cure for military fever. That much they did promise. And they can do it. You said that yourself. Even if they can't bring me back, nobody will die from it again. That's worth something, Owen."

"Yes. Something. So that's the price NAC is willing to pay for a guinea pig—" The intercom buzzed. Bundy glared at it as though he had never seen one before. "I told you not to interrupt me," he snapped into the box. Then he shrugged helplessly as he listened to the message. "Nancy, your husband is outside. Do you want to see him?"

"Yes, in a minute. Just let me pull myself together."

"I'll say one thing for this horrible business. At least it's brought you two closer together. How does John feel about cryonics? Surely as a doctor he can't have much faith in it."

Nancy broke into a low, mirthless laugh. "Owen, you should have seen some of the ridiculous things he's had faith in over the years. Fat farms, golden-age computer dating, dial-a-doctor. We were almost broke, living off my salary, until he finally got the job at NAC. He wants me to do it. But I think that's because he loves me, and he's scared. John's the kind of man who can make himself believe anything he wants."

Her statement confirmed Bundy's own judgment. As often as he tried to be broad-minded, he had no use for John Victor or for any other doctor who would employ his talents and training to play the glad-handed huckster for a medical-supply company. Mostly, he decided, he resented Victor because he had married Nancy. Why couldn't she see through that glib, good-looking Southern phony? he had wondered a hundred times. She could have had any man she wanted. Why John Victor? Finally, for want of any choice, he had thrown up his hands and accepted the marriage as one of life's nasty little tricks. He turned sharply to the intercom.

"Please ask Dr. Victor to come in."

John Victor almost had not come. But the idea of his wife spending more then five minutes alone with Owen Bundy was more than he could stand. No arguments, he resolved, no matter what the old bastard says. Don't force Nancy into choosing sides. You'll lose that one hands down. Just be sweet and concerned. He was careful to affect his most doleful mien before opening the door to Bundy's office.

"Nancy, darling, I took a chance that you might be here. I've got good news for you."

Nancy watched him cross the room in three long strides. He paused only for a curt nod to Bundy. Then he sat down beside her on the sofa and took both her hands in his.

"Your mother's arrived a week early. She's at the apartment right now, waiting for you. I must say, she was very upset that you weren't at home to meet her."

Nancy's heart sank. She knew she should feign a smile, or at least make the effort. Suddenly all the medical reports and glum-faced doctors disappeared from her mind. This reality was even harder to swallow. Her mother had come to watch her only child die, then to bring the body home. First her father, now her. Wetness blurred her vision. She tasted salt on her tongue.

"I thought you'd be happy," Victor said innocently. Then he turned to Bundy. "I thought she'd be happy."

Nancy painfully straighted her knees and pulled herself to her feet. "We'd better be going, John. Thank you again, Owen."

Bundy hurried to help Nancy with her coat. "Please, dear . . ." he whispered in her ear. "Don't make any important decisions without speaking to me. Call me any hour, night or day."

"I will, Owen," she answered without hearing him. Her mind was on the meeting that awaited her just a few miles away.

They were in the car before Victor spoke again.

"Nancy, I don't understand you," he said in his most exasperated tone. "I thought you loved your mother. I thought you'd be delighted to see her. But instead of smiles, you burst into tears. And in front of a stranger. Whatever will Dr. Bundy think of you?"

The walk down Bundy's short hallway and out to the street had sapped the last of Nancy's strength. She sank back in her seat and watched the crowds laden with brightly wrapped Christmas packages. They overflowed the sidewalks, spilling out into the streets to further snarl the midtown traffic. This time she was glad it would take an extra fifteen minutes to get home.

"I know you don't understand me, John," she said without condemnation. It amazed her that for at least two years of her adult life she had actually believed that John Victor was an intelligent, sensitive man. Perhaps, she reasoned, it was because he looked so intelligent and sensitive. His fine features and crisp blue eyes should have fooled her for a week, or a month. But years? God, you must have been crazy. It was just that he should have been so much better. She remembered him as a young officer in his starched white Navy uniform carefully browsing through a rack of dusty wine bottles behind the counter.

She watched him until the clerk, who knew her from the checks she cashed, noticed her curiosity.

"Dr. Victor is quite an expert," he told her. "We let him have samples for the wine-tasting course he teaches."

Then Victor turned around and caught her eye. She was momentarily embarrassed.

"How about a bold yet sassy claret?" was the first thing to pop into her head. Why didn't you just keep your mouth shut? she wondered in retrospect.

"John, don't you realize that Mother's come to bury me?"

"Well, I didn't . . ." he stammered.

"Forget it, John. Do me a favor. Call Dr. Stepp and find out when he could take me in. He did say that I should be under observation before . . . you know. Jesus, I haven't got the strength to spend the rest of my time alone with Mother."

"Of course I will." Victor tempered his enthusiasm. "As soon as I get back to my office."

"Please don't forget."

Victor waited until he saw the doorman scurrying out to meet the car. Then he leaned over and kissed Nancy lightly on the cheek.

"I'll be home early as I can, dear. Give my love to Mother."

He began rolling the moment Nancy was inside, but only as far as the corner phone booth. He was far too excited to spend the forty minutes it would take driving across town to NAC's New York headquarters. He reached Stepp on his private phone.

Bill Addison found himself at the end of a long line of dour men in white coats. Up ahead he could see the window where half a dozen at a time were allowed to pause for a look. When their minute was up, an usher would hand them each an NAC press release and point the way to a meeting room at the end of the hall. He appreciated the organization involved. NAC was good at that sort of thing. The press had had their turn the day before; now it was the doctors. Will it be the Boy Scouts tomorrow? he wondered. The line moved steadily, by increments of six steps, toward the window. An usher moved in behind him. He was the last member of the next group.

The doctors ahead were chatting amiably, like strangers at a museum who had just discovered a common interest. Their talk was frivolous, and Addison felt himself growing angry. They gawked while he tried to pay his respects in the middle of a three-ring circus. The obituary stuck in his mind. Three lines disposed of Nancy Seymour. Not so much as a grave site or "in lieu of flowers," so he knew where to find her. He told himself that it didn't matter. Dead was dead whether they shovel in the dirt or spread the ashes. In a way, he was glad she had chosen cryonic suspension. He would see her one more time.

The line moved. Suddenly Addison was pressed against the cold glass. He saw Nancy across twenty feet of frozen mist. She stood upright, like a mummy in a sarcophagus of gleaming chromium steel that bared her face and shoulders through a plexiglass shield. They had captured her like a butterfly in a moment of peace. Addison strained his eyes, but still she looked no more dead then a person asleep. He wanted to pound on the glass and cry out to her.

"Doctor, doctor . . . is anything wrong?" the usher asked politely. Addison looked up sharply. The rest of his group was already well down the corridor.

"No," he answered in a whisper. "What could possibly be wrong?"

8

Nancy felt the hot lights soak through her skin and burn behind her eyes. She was lost in a vast, empty desert in a dream with a life of its own. She wanted desperately to wake up. She tried to shout, but her throat was so dry that her tongue stuck in her mouth. The buzzing around her head sharpened until she knew it was voices. People were reaching out to her. She had to open her eyes. The light came from directly overhead. Everything around it was black as night. She blinked and gasped for air. Then she heard the shouts like a roll of thunder.

"She's alive," echoed a chorus of voices.

"Nancy, it's me, John. You've made it."

John Victor's face hovered just above her. She tried to speak but she could feel sleep pulling her back like quicksand. She managed to turn her head slightly to see the sunlight that poured in through the large window beside her bed. Then she smiled at the doctors who surrounded her bed.

"Just rest now, darling. You'll be fine," Victor said softly. He continued to hold her hand until she drifted back to sleep. Then all at once his elation burst the boundaries of restraint. He threw his arms in the air and shouted.

"We did it. She's alive."

The doctors erupted into a cheer. They had come in from all over the hospital. Even the largest room on the floor was barely sufficient to hold them, and the bouquets of flowers that covered every inch of table and windowsill space. A nurse pushed brusquely through the crowd to check the IV tubes in Nancy's arms.

"I think that's quite enough excitement for now," she said. "Miss Seymour needs her rest."

Sour old bitch, Victor thought, but he continued to beam. The other doctors took their cue from the nurse and began to slip out of the room. Victor wanted to join them. He was tired after two days in the hospital. But he had been the first to arrive and was determined to be the last to leave. He slumped into a chair beside Nancy's bed. It was a fine idea, he thought, bringing her to Metropolitan Hospital to recover. Let the world watch her recovery. Of course, we could have handled it up at NAC, but if cryonics is going to be believable, it must be out front, and public. Victor wished the idea had been his instead of Stepp's. Still, he thought, rising from his comfortable chair, there're some things that even Stepp can't do. I'm her husband. He straightened his tie as he watched the barges creeping up the sun-drenched East River six floors below. The view reminded him that Nancy had always preferred the summertime. Wake up in the season of your choice, he thought. There's a slogan with an honest ring.

Both the cops on duty sat up as Victor opened the door to the corridor. A crowd was waiting. He spotted the bank of television cameras and began to smile. Flashbulbs popped in his face. He tried to pick out a sensible question from the barrage of shouts. Microphones were thrust in his face. Most of the newsmen looked like they had spent the night in the corridor. Victor knew they hadn't waited that long to be given a brushoff.

"We know your wife's alive, Dr. Victor. Can you tell us how the NAC cryonics process works?"

Victor felt like talking. He enjoyed the attention. That was just as Stepp had foreseen. His warning rang in Victor's brain: Keep your mouth shut.

"Gentlemen, I'm very tired, and relieved—"

"When can we see Nancy?"

Victor recognized his questioner. He was an eager young man who had worked with Nancy.

"Soon, very soon. The minute we're sure her military fever is in remission. We're just as anxious to have her up and around as you are to see her, but you must understand that Nancy is the first human recipient of the antitoxin serum we've developed. Of course, it's been extensively tested on animals, with very positive results. Still, there's always the chance of complications or unforeseen side effects." He made sure his voice carried a strong tremor of concern. In his heart he felt nothing but joy. He knew for a positive fact that the serum would work.

The reporters began to buzz among themselves. A moment later Victor could have been standing naked in the corridor. The entire pack was moving as one man toward the other end of the hall. He tried to look over their heads and past the tangle of electronic equipment. The elevator door had opened. Suddenly he understood. The journalists had just been killing time with him. Dr. Stepp had arrived. Victor felt the edge of his elation fade. He wanted to storm away, if only to see if anyone would notice. Instead, he joined the crowd of reporters. Although Victor had seen him only once before, he instantly recognized the man at Stepp's side. It was the boss, Arch Kholer, carrying a large bouquet of flowers.

Now he was stuck. He did not know whether he was expected to join Kholer or remain quietly in the background. The reporters were packed in tight, and it was difficult for him to maneuver through their ranks. He stood on his toes to catch Stepp's eye, but all he could see was the top of his bald head reflecting back the camera's lights. He was beginning to feel like a fool. Then, to his total surprise and delight, Kholer stepped past the reporters to greet him. Victor took his extended hand and clutched it like a life rope. His embarrassment turned to gratitude and he beamed as he drank in Kholer's praise and recognition.

"John, my friend, this is your victory too." Kholer laid his other hand on Victor's shoulder and practically dragged him through the last row of reporters. "More for you than any of us."

Victor clearly recalled their only previous meeting, a year and a half before. Kholer had walked in on a cocktail party his hospital-products division had thrown to celebrate a large order. He shook hands with everyone, including the waiters, offered one inspirational toast, wished the assembled a prosperous year, and left. Suddenly I'm his dear friend, Victor thought with satisfaction. He must really have big plans for cryonics.

Kholer shook his head supportively while Stepp continued his statement to the press.

". . . So while we have every confidence in the serum, it will take at least a week before we can effect a positive remission of the damage already done. Until then, Miss Seymour will continue on life-support systems and be unavailable for questions. I'm sure we're all anxious to know what's waiting for us on the other side, eh, gentlemen?" Stepp winked into the nearest camera. "But as to the details of NAC's cryonic process, or at what point in the process we began to administer the serum, why, you could just as well ask Coke for their secret formula. We have no objection to scientific verification of what we've accomplished. But I'm afraid that for the present we'll keep the 'how' to ourselves."

Stepp held up both his hands in a clear gesture that the press conference was over.

"Gentlemen, please," he shouted over the din of more questions. "We must look in on Miss Seymour."

Victor felt Stepp's hand on his arm as he ushered him back toward Nancy's room. Halfway down the corridor the policemen moved between them and the reporters, protecting their rear flank. Suddenly it was quiet again. Stepp led them into an empty room beside Nancy's. It was crammed with the overflow of her flowers and smelled like a hothouse gone to seed. Victor noticed that the bed was rumpled and the ashtrays piled with cigar butts. The cops had been cooping on the job. Stepp turned on the air conditioner full blast. Then Victor noticed a fourth man in the room. His face was vaguely familiar, but he could not recall the name. Stepp moved between them and gestured at the tall, thin, beak-nosed man.

"John, this is Eric Jason, NAC's director of public relations." Stepp spat out the title like an epithet. Jason ignored the coldness of the introduction and Victor managed a friendly smile. Whatever Stepp's public attitude, they both knew that publicity was a job that needed doing if cryonics was going to pay for itself. After a perfunctory shake of Victor's hand, Jason turned his full attention to Arch Kholer.

"Well, Arch," he said proudly. "Not too shabby for opening day. I told you the press would eat it up. More good news, Nancy will be on the cover of *People* next week. Cryonics was one humanitarian gesture that will turn a fine profit. John, got something for you, too." He passed a bulky envelope to Victor. "Here's a schedule of Nancy's appearances for the next month. *Today* show. *Good Morning America*, Merv, Carson, all the hot spots. You, John, will sit quietly at her side. . . . Quietly at her side."

"Just one bloody minute, Eric," Stepp cut in. "You're not going to make a circus out of this. I won't allow it. Cryonics is my department."

"Of course it is, Amos." Kholer laid his hand gently on Stepp's shoulder. "And don't think I'm not impressed by all you've accomplished. But you must admit that it has been expensive. You've had your free hand, just as I promised, but first-half earnings are going to look like hell. You know it would have been much easier on us financially if you'd taken an extra six months to find a cure instead of that expensive crash program you initiated. But that's the way you wanted it, and cryonics is your department. However, Amos, there are some hard realities in this world. Hardest among them are stockholders. All Eric wants to do is put our best face forward."

"He's a whore," Stepp snapped. "Arch, I'm surprised at you. How could you consider scrimping where human life is involved? Of course I've no objection to public airing of cryonics. I welcome it. But with dignity."

Jason brushed Stepp aside. "Arch, dignity is a luxury NAC can't afford right now. Dr. Stepp saw to that with his billion-dollar experiment. Thank God it worked, or we'd all be out on the street. I daresay Nancy will be dying to tell her story. Let her. Encourage her. Arch, we've cast our bread upon the waters and it will come back in great waves of green. Just wait until Nancy starts talking for herself. The world is going to fall in love with our Sleeping Beauty."

9

Bill Addison read four separate accounts of the story as he finished breakfast in his Washington apartment. The accounts were almost identical, but his interest never flagged. He found himself smiling each time Nancy's name was mentioned. Only the photograph upset him. He knew exactly where it had been taken. He had stood in the same spot himself, peering through the glass at Nancy's frozen death-mask face. The memory made him shiver.

He almost jumped at the sound of the house phone.

"Mr. Addison, this is Jerry. Your cab's out front. Better hurry. I hear the traffic out to Dulles is terrible this morning."

"Thanks. Tell the driver I'll be down in a minute." He made a mental note to tip the doorman an extra dollar while he quickly stuffed the newspapers into his already bulging briefcase. There would be plenty of time to study them on the flight to Bonn. He walked around his small apartment making a ritualistic check to be certain that all the lights were off and the plants properly moist. It was part of his routine and he did it without thinking. For a moment he wondered whether he should go ahead with this trip to Germany. Maybe Nancy would need him in New York.

What the hell's wrong with you? Addison wondered. The woman you love is alive. You should be doing cartwheels. Instead, you're depressed. Why? Because she dumped you to go back to her husband? Because you thought cryonics was a lot of bullshit and you don't like being wrong?

Suddenly Addison felt a wave of relief. You'll see her again, he decided, the minute she's recovered. What she said before was part of the sickness. All that's changed now. He spent the time in the cab wondering how soon he could get in touch with her. It was all he could do to keep from phoning her from the airport. Only the sure knowledge that someone else would answer the phone and insist on taking a message stopped him. He could wait a little longer. Then they would be together. He was as sure of it as anything in his life.

Nothing hurt. Nancy stretched her arms. The pain in her joints was almost gone. She could move her shoulders without wincing. It was as though a suit of armor had been removed from her body. The tubes in her nose and arms had disappeared. All she could think of was a barefoot run on the beach. She watched her mother rearranging the bouquets of flowers that ran the length of the windowsill. Her small, plump fingers busily flicked tiny dust particles off the petals while turning the pots that fraction of an inch to maximize their exposure to the sun.

"Did you find out when I can leave, Mother? The doctors won't tell me a thing."

Lois Seymour carefully set down a vase and turned her cherubic face toward her daughter. Even after a week she still had difficulty believing that Nancy was truly alive. She was elated, and made no effort to hide it. Joy seemed to exude through the pores of her skin and laughter bubble into every word.

She had never come to view her daughter in the tank. Not that she had opposed the cryonic experiment; she simply looked on it as a noble contribution to science. She did not have the slightest expectation that Nancy would live again. To see her frozen would have been far too painful.

"Doctors never tell you anything," Lois Seymour answered. "But it's clear to me that you're coming along just fine. I'll bet you're out in a week."

"I've got to get out. God, I feel like I've missed so much already."

"You should count your blessings, young lady. You've missed nothing but a nasty, cold winter. And the doctors know best, your husband among them. I hope you realize just how lucky you are to have a man who loves you the way John does. Do you know that he phoned me once a week while you were . . . you know . . . just to talk about you?"

"Yes." Nancy's tone softened. "John can be very considerate."

Lois checked the wall clock. "There's something I want to watch on television."

"Not another program on cryonics, Mother. You've seen ten of them already. Isn't anybody talking about anything else?"

"No, they're not," Lois said. "And I haven't seen this one yet."

"Well, if it's on at two-thirty in the afternoon on a Wednesday, it can't be very important."

"Hush." Lois snapped on the set.

Nancy watched the zoom shot behind the opening credits as the picture tightened on her frozen chamber. The first time she had seen the shot, it frightened her. Now she found it mildly amusing, like the opening of an ancient horror movie. She studied herself critically. The flesh-colored protective masking over her hair and eyebrows lent a ghostly, unfinished quality to her features. She was glad she had no memory of it. Her time in the tank did not exist as a part of her life. Even when she saw the films, she felt that it all could have been happening to someone else.

Her last memory of the event was a burst of pain. John was there, she remembered, and the nurses; perhaps other doctors, too. They were all hurrying. Nancy couldn't see them clearly. The respirator had blocked her view. She gasped, and they had given her drugs to help her breathe. There was fear. She knew she was dying. All their faces told her that much. Their frantic efforts were intended, she knew, to keep her alive as long as possible before the freezing process began. Why? she had wondered vaguely through her veil of pain. All this to satisfy some legal requirement. She couldn't remember if it had gone on for days, or only hours. Then the last wave of pain crashed against her body and she remembered nothing. Now, here she was, in a different place, in a different time sequence. That part of it still unnerved her a bit. You were dead, she told herself. The hereafter is here and now.

"That's where you've got those little scars, dear." Nancy heard her mother's sympathetic voice. "It's not so bad. Nobody but your husband will ever see them."

"Oh, Mother!"

But Nancy watched the animated presentation with more than usual interest. The film had been prepared by NAC. She found her hand wandering to the small dot of scar tissue under her left breast. The figure on the screen had a similar mark, and another like Nancy's three inches below her navel. Those were the points where tubes were inserted to draw out the body's blood and fluids.

"DMSO is a sophisticated anticoagulant drug . . ." the narrator droned on. Antifreeze, Nancy thought.

"Turn it off, Mom. I've seen enough for today. It's starting to get on my nerves."

Lois reluctantly clicked off the set. "You're so on edge today," she said.

"I guess I am. It's just that I'm feeling tried and . . ." Suddenly she wanted to be alone.

"I can take a hint. I'll call later, dear."

"Thanks, Mom."

"If you're up to it, it would be nice if you answered some of your mail." She pointed at the small mountain of cards and letters on the table beside the bed. "All those people have been so kind and thoughtful. . . ."

"I'll get right to it."

Nancy could barely wait until her mother was out the door before she picked up the phone. Her fingers drummed restlessly on the night table until she finally got her party.

"Matt Sharp," she snapped at the voice at the other end. "I'm not dead anymōre. Why don't you return my calls?"

"Still as sweet as ever, I see. How the hell are you?"

"If you really cared, you'd have called."

"I did. About six times. It's impossible to get a line into your room. They kept telling me you can't receive any calls. What's up, anyway?"

"Jesus. That sounds like John's doing. He's trying to protect me, I suppose. Actually, I'm feeling fine. Can you come over? I'm sick of talking to nurses."

"Sure. If they'll let me in."

"Tell them you're my brother. Or kick the door down. I'd really love to see you."

"Me too, and what a sneaky way to scoop all the papers. You really are hot stuff. I'll see you right after we sign off tonight."

Two more weeks, Nancy thought excitedly. August 1 would be a fine day to start working again. They can't possibly keep me here more than another week. Then a few days at home to rest up and get myself together. I feel great already! It's time to start over again.

Nancy knew she had several hours to pass until Matt Sharp would arrive. She reluctantly glanced at the unopened mail on her table. It was divided into two stacks of about equal height. One consisted of personal letters and the other of business propositions. The latter were the ones she resented. A few were legitimate enough: offers to appear on television or speak to groups about what they frequently referred to as her "great experience." She answered the first few, thanking them for their interest and explaining that there simply was no "experience" that she could recall. If there had been, she, as a professional journalist, would have been the first to report it.

The majority of the business letters were easy to ignore. It wasn't that simple, however, with the personal letters. Most came from desperate people, families with a loved one about to die. They were looking for hope that Nancy could not give them. After a while she could almost sense the message from the postmark and handwriting on the envelope. She resolved to read them all, and answer them as best she could.

The knock came unexpectedly. She sat up in bed and put aside her letters.

"Come in."

The door swung open and Nancy beamed with delight.

"Matt, how wonderful to see you. Come in. Come in."

Sharp's warm embrace almost lifted Nancy out of bed. Then he planted a friendly wet kiss on her cheek. She could smell his acrid cigar smoke, but for once it didn't bother her a bit.

"Hey!" Sharp exclaimed, stepping back to examine her.

"You look great. What's all this crap about an approved-visitors list? I almost had to walk in backward so they'd think I was leaving."

Nancy wrinkled her brow. "I don't know what you mean. Unless . . ." John or perhaps Dr. Stepp ordered it, she thought. She would ask John about it the next time she saw him. "Now, tell me how you've managed without me," she said.

Sharp shrugged his broad shoulders and smiled sheepishly. "Not too bad. Everything's fine. That's why I could get here so early. Marsha's just about running the show for me. When can you come down for a visit?"

Nancy cringed inside. An invitation to visit was not what she had expected. That isn't what he really meant, she thought. Matt never could phrase things tactfully.

"I was thinking about August 1."

"That'll be just fine, Nancy. I'll tell the whole gang. We can all have lunch—"

"Lunch? Matt, I'm talking about my job. I want to start working on August 1. I expect to be out of here in another week, and that will give me a week to settle some personal . . ." Her voice trailed off as she watched Sharp pull himself slowly from his chair. His smile had faded and his head began to shake from side to side.

"That's what I was afraid of, Nancy. It's not that easy. Sure, we all want you back. You were great, you know that. But it's not that easy. We've hired someone to take your slot. Then there's the budget problem. You know how tough it is to take somebody on in mid-season."

"Cut it *out*, Matt," Nancy snapped. "None of those things would mean a damn if you really wanted me back. What's the matter?"

"I'm sorry. I shouldn't have tried to run one past you. Haven't you turned on a television set since your reanimation?"

"Well, certainly, but—"

"Don't you see, Nancy? *You're* the news. Every time I turn around, I see your face on the tube. How can I have you reporting the news when you *are* the news? You try asking someone a question and they'll ask you one right back: 'What's it like to be dead?' I don't mean that you can never get back into broadcast journalism. But you're going to have to wait until this thing cools down. Meanwhile, I bet there are a million things you can do." He gestured at the stack of mail. "Books, television. Kid, you're hot stuff."

"Too hot for you, I see," Nancy said bleakly. "Matt, it's not the money. Sure I can make a bundle right now, but that's not my career. It's not fair!"

"No, it's not," Sharp agreed. "But life isn't always fair. Nancy, I want you to know that we still love you. All of us. I want you to stay in touch." Sharp was halfway to the door when he stopped and turned around. Nancy could see the question forming on his lips, but he paused like a shy teenager asking for his first date.

"Nancy, I know you haven't spoken publicly yet. But for me, off the record, I promise . . . What's it really like to be dead?"

10

The corridor outside Nancy's room was 268 feet from the elevator to the window at the far end. She was sure she knew every cigarette burn along the length of the carpeted floor. Walking was part of her exercise, along with bends and stretches. She was growing stronger by the day. She could feel her progress and it gave her reason to work still harder. One more day, she thought, then I'll be released. Or I'll damned well walk out, she added angrily. She was still frowning when she passed the policeman posted in front of her door. He bounced to his feet.

"Is something wrong, Miss Seymour?"

"No, Ralph." She caught herself and began to smile. "I guess I'm just anxious to be leaving."

"I don't blame you a bit," the young officer answered thoughtfully, rubbing his pink chin. "Two weeks in this place is plenty. But you've been through an awful lot, and these doctors here know what's best. Wanna play a couple of hands of gin rummy?"

"Not right now, thanks. I've got to make a few calls before . . ." Before John shows up at five-fifteen on the dot, dependable as clockwork. Not exciting, but dependable. ". . . dinner."

"Sure, maybe later. I'd like a chance to get back my eight bucks."

"Later it is."

Nancy closed the door. She was half-hoping that John would arrive early. The tightness in her stomach told her that she was primed for an argument. She knew she was angry, but she couldn't put her finger on exactly why. John had been so reasonable, so damned reasonable, she fumed. Even the "approved-visitors list" was reasonable. She remembered how he whipped it out from among the thick sheaf of papers that comprised her chart. The list included practically every name she could recall.

"Nancy, we didn't want the press hounding you," Victor patiently explained. "On top of them, you'd have every huckster and fast-buck artist in New York pounding down your door. I'm sorry we forgot about your friends at the station."

Nancy wanted to shout. But that would have been petulant and immature. So instead she said, "I'm sorry, John."

"Well, I've some good news for you, darling. You can go home in a few days."

"A few days? John, I'd like to know why I'm still here. I feel fine. Besides, it isn't fair for me to take up a whole floor in a hospital."

John slid his dinner tray to the side and clasped his hands in front of him like an exasperated teacher forced to deal with the class dunce.

"Dr. Stepp and I know you feel fine, and we're both delighted. But even though our cure for military fever appears to have taken, you must remember that you are the first human subject. We have to be very careful about side effects or reactions to the medication. That's why you're still here, Nancy. Surely you can appreciate . . ."

"Yes, John, I appreciate it," Nancy replied sarcastically.

He had it coming, she thought. He didn't have to be quite so pompous. She began leafing through a listing of the evening's television programs. There wasn't one on cryonics. There hadn't been one the previous night either. Only two all week. You wait, Matt Sharp, the public has a very short memory. In six months nobody will even remember my name. Her eyes fell on her address book propped up beside the telephone. For a moment it seemed to her that the people who mattered had already forgotten. Nobody likes hospitals.

If you were really sick, you wouldn't notice. But she did notice, and it bothered her.

What's changed? she asked herself. She suspected that she already knew the answer, and she didn't like it one bit. She had detected a pattern to her friends' visits. They would start off all right, calling and wanting to come in. Then they would look her over and see that she was fine. From that point on they all seemed ill-at-ease. Even Mother was never comfortable for more than a half-hour, she recalled. At least Matt asked the right question. Perhaps you remind them that everybody's going to die. "Forget it," she snapped out loud. It'll be different once you're out of here. Life will get back to normal.

Suddenly she burst out laughing. But there were tears in her eyes. Normal! You were dead for six months and eight days. Nothing about you qualifies as normal, not any longer. She lay down on the freshly made bed and stared at the ceiling. Then she rolled over and watched the sluggish river traffic and the smoke rising from the factories in Queens, on the far side of the river. Dark thunderclouds were gathering. All at once she felt very tired.

A shrill scream of terror tore through Nancy's door. The startled cop jumped out of his chair. A moment later, two nurses were running toward him. Just behind them an orderly, hunched forward like a bobsled starter, pushed a rattling cart of emergency equipment. The P.A. barked out calls for doctors. Nancy's screams rang in Ralph Herman's ears as he wrenched at the doorknob. He stopped cold. The door was locked. He twisted the knob again, almost violently. It would not budge.

"She's locked it from the inside. I'll get Maintenance." The nurse turned back toward her station.

"No time for that bullshit," Herman said emphatically.

He took two quick steps back and flung his shoulder forward against the soft wood door. It flew open with a crash of splintered panels. The momentum carried him halfway across the room, almost to the edge of Nancy's bed. He looked straight into her eyes. They were glassy and wide with fear. Her skin was clammy white. It was a look he had seen often enough before on the streets. She sat perfectly still, arms clasped in front of her body. Beads of cold sweat ran down her forehead.

"Nancy," he said softly. "Can you hear me, kid? Are you okay?"

The nurses pushed past him. They began to massage her wrists. Herman could tell they were worried. Then Nancy blinked, and gasped like she had just come up from underwater.

John Victor stood motionless in the doorway. The nurses stopped their work the moment they noticed him. His face was purple with rage. "What the hell's going on in here?" He could barely control the tremor in his voice.

"Dr. Victor, I . . . we were just . . ."

"It's all right, John." Nancy's voice came out in a scratchy whisper. "I was having a nightmare. I'm fine now. Really."

"Her pulse is slowing down now, Doctor. It's almost normal," a nurse cut in. "And her color's starting to come back."

"Thank you," Victor said curtly. "Contact Dr. Stepp immediately. We won't need that." He waved away the orderly's cart. "Now, please leave us alone."

Herman turned to go with the others. Only the touch of Victor's hand on his arm stopped him.

"You were the first one inside, Officer?" Victor whispered, nodding at the remnants of the door.

"Yes, Doctor. I heard your wife's screams and the door was locked so I had to—"

"Thank you, Officer . . ."

"Herman."

"Please wait for me outside. I want to talk with you privately." Then he nodded his head to dismiss the policeman. All the while he spoke, he hadn't taken his finger off Nancy's pulse.

"You're very agitated," he said softly, looking into her eyes. "What happened, darling?"

"Nothing. Really, John, it was just a bad dream." Nancy forced herself to smile. "Why, I can't even remember what it was all about. Everybody has bad dreams once in a while."

"Of course they do," Victor replied noncommittally.

Nancy sensed that her chance of leaving in the morning was slipping through her fingers. She got off the bed and began pacing the length of the room. The sight of the broken door upset her, as though the jagged splinters of wood were clear evidence of her continuing illness.

"I'm fine, John," she blurted out. "I want to go home."

Victor shrugged. "In the morning, as we agreed."

Nancy felt a wave of relief pass through her body. She was going home. That was the important thing.

"What can you tell me about this nightmare?" Victor asked casually.

Nancy tried to concentrate. She vaguely felt that cooperating would be repayment for keeping his word. After a moment she shook her head blankly. "I don't remember anything. Just the fear I felt when I awoke. It was childish, I suppose."

"Perhaps," Victor answered with little conviction. Then his mood changed. "I've a surprise for you. No more hospital meals. I'm giving you a taste of the outside world. Tonight we're dining on lobster and champagne. You get yourself ready. I'll see to the cart."

"Lobster! That's wonderful, John." Nancy threw her arms around Victor's shoulders and kissed him. He smiled shyly as he shifted out of her embrace.

"I'll be right back, Nancy. I ought to look in on the nurses, too, put their minds at ease. They were very upset, you know."

As Victor had hoped, Officer Herman was waiting for him halfway down the corridor.

"How's your wife feeling?" he asked solicitously as Victor approached.

"Much better, thank you. Officer, can you recall what Nancy was screaming? Did she say anything you could make out?"

"No," Herman answered thoughtfully after a moment. Then a puzzled look crossed his face. "Yeah, it sounded like 'I'm alive. I'm alive.' Hey, could that have something to do with her comin' back from the dead?"

"Don't ask me," Victor said curtly. "I'm an internist, not a shrink."

"Remember, you don't have to speak to them," Victor said soothingly. Nancy found his attitude annoying. She still felt more like one of "them."

"John, the press has a right to my story. You've protected me for weeks. Enough is enough."

She wished she felt as self-confident as she sounded. You've got to finish it, she thought. Answer every question. Then the story can fade away.

She could see the crowd in front of her building from a block off. They packed the entire width of the sidewalk. Cables and electronic gear trailed into the remote units double-parked along half the length of the street. Somebody spotted the long black NAC limo. In a moment the crowd of reporters was poised at the edge of the curb. The doorman vainly tried to maintain some semblance of order. It was too late for that. Nancy heard her name shouted by a dozen people as the car eased to a stop. They barely gave her room to open the door. Her burly driver pushed clear a path to the building entrance.

"Get back," he bellowed. "Can't you see the lady ain't well yet?"

The reporters ignored him. Nancy quickly picked out a number of familiar faces. Then she heard a question she liked. She stepped out of the car and paused until the reporters quieted down.

"You bet my life's changed since the operation," she answered. "Before this, you guys wouldn't even buy me a cup of coffee. Now look at you, hanging on my every word. Really, there's nothing to it. As far as I'm concerned, the entire six months I was in the tank never even happened."

Her eyes wandered from face to face as she spoke. She had already begun phrasing a response to the next question. All at once she felt as comfortable as if she were still on the other side of the cameras.

"My doctors assure me that my military fever is cured. The disease has been conquered forever. . . ." A face caught her eye. She looked again but it was gone, like a puff of smoke in a strong wind. A cold chill shot through her stomach. She had never seen him before, she was sure of it. Yet . . .

"Nancy, would you recommend this cryonics process for other terminally ill people?" The question was like a morning shower. She snapped back and focused on the nearest camera.

Willie Garvin turned for a last look, but even the wisps of Nancy's blond hair were blocked by the taller men who surrounded her. Stupid, he thought with rage, stupid, stupid. He slapped his fist into his open palm and continued to mumble all the way to Madison Avenue. Yet he had to admit that he felt much better. If you really love someone, he reasoned, then seeing her is worth any risk.

11

"Welcome home!" Lois Seymour exclaimed as she flung open the door. Her freshly curled white hair sparkled under the hallway light and all her teeth showed in a wide smile as she spread her arms in greeting. Her hug lifted Nancy off the ground. She was far stronger than her matronly shape should have allowed. "Now I know you're really cured," she bubbled.

"I'm fine, Mom," Nancy answered, warmly squeezing Lois' hand. Then she froze in true surprise. The apartment in front of her was not her own. Her eyes darted from the spot where her white sofa had been, across a tweed carpet that was yet to feel the bottom of a shoe, to a sedate background of dark green drapes. Suddenly she became aware of John's body close behind her and the weight of his hands on her shoulders.

"What do you think, darling?" he whispered in her ear.

Nancy moved forward, out of his grasp. She had no idea what to think. The surprise took her breath away.

"Lois helped me pick it all out," John continued enthusiastically. He took Nancy's hand and led her into the living room. She could barely contain her urge to rush forward and examine every piece. It was all new, yet familiar as an old tune. Then she realized why.

"My scrapbook. John, these are special things. How did you know?"

The scrapbook was something she had never shown him. Mostly, she had cut and pasted during slow times at the station. It was in the box she had brought home, along with her address books. That's where the names on his hospital list came from, she thought. He searched my stuff. The idea annoyed her for only a moment. Why not? I was dead. Maybe I had money stashed away someplace.

"It wasn't hard," Victor said modestly, kissing Nancy's cheek. "You circled all your favorites, remember, darling. All Mother and I had to do was figure out how to get it into one apartment."

"It's incredible," she allowed.

"There's more on the way. Why don't you fix us a drink? I'll put your bags away," Victor said as he walked off toward the bedrooms.

"Don't I get to look at the rest of the place?" Nancy called after him.

"One surprise at a time."

Nancy saw the smug look in her mother's eyes and responded with a smile. She knew just what was coming. The thought made her pour an extra measure of Scotch into the silver tumbler.

"Do you have any idea how much money he spent on this place?" Lois whispered conspiratorially. "Why, the paint alone cost—"

"Mother," Nancy cut in. "That's not important. You're so materialistic." She quickly softened her tone in response to the hurt look in Lois' eyes. "All right, tell me, how much did it cost?"

Lois looked around quickly, seeking some particular item to launch her discourse.

"A fortune. Why, the carpet alone was almost twenty thousand dollars. If money could buy happiness—"

"—and turtles could fly."

"Sit down, dear." Lois gestured at the plush red velvet sofa. She handed Nancy her Scotch from the dry sink bar. Nancy realized it was the first time her mother had ever done

that. She accepted the drink. "Don't you think I've got eyes
in my head?"

"What are you talking about, Mother?"

"John. He's a very sensitive man. He loves you very much.
All this was his way of asking for a fresh start. I know there
have been problems between you two. But maybe now that
we've had one miracle, things can be the way they were in
the good days."

The words struck a chord in Nancy's heart. She could
barely remember that there ever were any good days. The
John that came to mind was cold and arrogant. She had been
one small step from walking out. But perhaps he's changed,
she thought. Perhaps seven bad years could be wiped away
and her husband could once again be the handsome young
doctor with such bright prospects. The same man who had
first caught her eye. Perhaps cryonics is the smash success
he's needed all his life. Not that it's really his, she knew well
enough. Cryonics belongs to Amos Stepp. John just carries
his briefcase, but that is as close as he's ever gotten. Maybe it
will be enough. She thought of Bill Addison, and the comparison brought her a pang of sadness. She realized that it did
not matter very much what John did. Whatever gratitude she
might feel, she could never again love him.

"It's certainly something to hope for," Nancy said wistfully.

"Nancy, I've watched John for the past eight months. I've
never seen a more loving, caring husband. Now, why can't
you try to meet him halfway?" Lois' eyes flitted toward the
bedroom, and Nancy understood the meaning of "halfway."

"Mother, I know what you're getting at. Please don't rush
me."

"Why not? What's wrong with the word 'grandchild'?" she
said with a lump in her throat. "I thought you were going to
die, and I almost gave up hope. But now . . ."

"All right!" Nancy said in a voice that ends conversations.
"I'll try. That's all I can promise."

Lois' face brightened immediately. She dabbed her eyes,
but she was smiling. Nancy felt a burden of guilt lifted from
her shoulders. Lois suddenly bounced to her feet.

"John," she said warmly. "Come join us for a drink. We've
finished with all the girl talk."

"Good." Victor touched Nancy's hand as he passed.

"There's one more thing," Lois added. "John would be too modest to speak for himself. What he did to this apartment was an act of faith. That's right, faith, Nancy. Everybody, including me, thought you were gone. But not John. He went right ahead, just like he knew you would be coming home. He never lost his faith, and that gave me strength, too."

Nancy saw the moisture swell in her mother's eyes. Suddenly she was very proud of her husband.

"It's lovely, John. Really. It's exactly what I've always wanted. Thank you."

Victor leaned over and kissed her. "Now, Lois," he said. "You've got some explaining to do. What are those suitcases I saw in the foyer?"

"I'm going home," she answered firmly, folding her arms across her chest. "Nancy's fine now and I'm not a person to overstay her welcome. We've all got to start putting our lives back in order. I'd just be in the way here, John. It's settled. I leave on the ten-o'clock plane."

Nancy felt abandoned. She had not even considered the possibility that her mother would leave her so soon and she would be left alone with her husband. Somehow, it made her rather anxious.

"I don't agree with you, Lois. But I respect your feelings," Victor said with just the right touch of sadness in his voice. "I want you to know that you've always got a home with us."

Why couldn't I say that? Nancy thought as she saw the glow of pride and happiness spread across her mother's face. She half-expected to hear a ring of cynicism in Victor's tone, some trace of the man she thought she knew. Can someone change so completely? she wondered.

The apartment was dark, and very quiet. Nancy read the time off the luminous dial that cast a faint green light over the unfamiliar furniture beside her bed. It was after two A.M., but she was wide-awake. She knew there would be no sleep until she confronted her own disappointment. It wasn't supposed to be like this, she thought, remembering her first moments of elation when she awakened from the cryonic sleep. You had a second chance, and what has it become? New furniture; not a new life. Not even the same old life. You've lost your job and . . . Nancy sat up in bed and began to dab the wetness from her eyes. Bill Addison, she thought. You've lost him too. But he could have at least sent a card. Perfect strangers had done that much. Why should he? she thought sadly. You tossed him out of your life like a worn-out pair of shoes. At the time, it had seemed like such a fair and decent thing to do. No half-measures for you. Not Nancy Seymour. So now you need him and he's gone.

"Stop it," she shouted out loud. "You're wallowing in self-pity."

Then she held her breath, afraid she would hear the pounding of Victor's feet in the hallway. Nothing stirred. After a moment Nancy blew out a long sigh. Your life is a miracle and you're not going to squander it, she resolved. The good things will come. All at once she knew what she had to do. It seemed so obvious that she could scarcely believe it had not occurred to her sooner. She would tell John about it in the morning, after a good night's sleep.

12

John Victor set aside his newspaper. He made no effort to conceal the broad smile of satisfaction that spread quickly across his face.

Nancy's work schedule had been erratic for years, while Victor rose precisely at seven o'clock every morning. By tacit mutual agreement they had made a point of avoiding each other in the mornings. They had both found it the simplest way to start the day without an argument.

"Coffee, dear?" Victor asked to break the momentary silence. He really wanted to ask Nancy why she was dressed for work, looking as well-turned-out as she ever did in front of the cameras.

"Thanks, John. Have you got a few minutes? I'd like to talk."

"Of course."

Nancy sat down across the table. She looked straight into his eyes, but the words she had practiced stuck like a lump in her throat.

"I know I owe you a great deal, John. Perhaps my life. But what I feel is gratitude, not love. I don't know if that's a strong enough reason for a life together."

"I understand," Victor said solemnly.

Nancy's eyes widened in surprise.

"I've done everything I could to overcome my past mistakes," Victor continued. "But I love you, Nancy, and I want you to be happy. If there's another man, I'll move out. I can understand. God knows, I've given you cause."

"No," Nancy said quickly. The last thing she expected was her husband's acquiescence. "It's not that at all. You've been wonderful ever since the illness." Suddenly she found herself on the defensive, fighting back a surge of guilt. "I wasn't talking about leaving you now, John. I just wanted you to know how I felt. If you can put up with our odd living arrangement, I suppose I can too, for a little while, anyway."

"I'll go along with anything you decide to do," Victor said.

Nancy wondered why she didn't feel the gratitude Victor's understanding attitude should have evoked in her, but at the moment she had too many things to do. Sorting out her feelings would have to wait for later.

"I'm going to the studio this morning. I've got an idea I'd like to bat around with Matt. God, I feel like I've just gotten out of jail. By the way . . ." Nancy turned back from the door. "Where did you put my clothes? I could hardly find anything this morning, except for this outfit I'm wearing."

"I had to empty the closets for the painters anyway, so I thought I'd have everything cleaned. What with all the confusion the last couple of weeks, I just forgot to have it delivered. I'm sorry. I'll take care of it today."

The explanation sounded so reasonable that Nancy didn't give it another thought.

Nancy's worst fears quickly proved groundless. She moved practically unnoticed through the early-morning crowds. Occasionally a head would turn, or a pair of eyes linger a moment too long, but she knew it was little more than the attention given any attractive woman. Less, she judged, than in the period when she was appearing nightly on the news. Her pace gradually gained confidence. She began to enjoy the morning sun and found she could smile back at the people who caught her eye. The world hasn't changed, she thought with a wave of relief.

New York was bustling and alive, just as she remembered it. She turned the last corner, past the old-fashioned bank with its domed ceiling and marble columns. A moment later she was standing under the green awning of the RCA Building. It was nice to be home.

For an instant the newsroom seemed frozen in time. Then she began to see small changes. Desks had been moved and the large room was far quieter than she remembered. Her eyes followed the line of desks back from the far wall. It took her just a moment to find her own. A young man she didn't know was leafing through a stack of papers. The sight of his coffee cup causing a ring on the immitation wood surface irritated her.

"Nancy, is that you?" Marsha Ward had come off the elevator behind her. When Nancy turned around, they were close enough to touch. Marsha held out both her hands and Nancy took them. "I knew you couldn't stay away forever. Well, come on. You're not going to stand here all morning."

Nancy followed Marsha's brisk pace past the newsroom toward the production department. She waved and smiled at familiar faces, but Marsha didn't give her a moment to linger. She opened an office door and ushered Nancy inside.

Marsha answered the look of surprise on Nancy's face. "They've promoted me. Didn't I mention it when I called?"

"No . . . congratulations." Nancy was impressed. It was a real office, not a cubicle. It had a sofa and glass coffee table and two windows with a view of the skating rink. "What did you have to do to get all this?"

"I'll never tell. Really, Nan, I've just been so lucky. Matt was promoted to news director, so they made me the executive producer. Me!"

Nancy squeezed Marsha's hand. "That's wonderful. I'm so happy for you."

"I still pinch myself. Sit down. Let me get you some coffee, from my private executive coffee machine."

"You really have made the big time," Nancy said, only half-jokingly.

Marsha settled down behind her highly polished mahogany desk. "Nan, I don't know what's the matter with me, yakking on about myself. You look great. Really great. It's hard to believe that you were . . . so ill. And you've become quite a celebrity."

"Not really," Nancy answered cautiously. "You know how people forget. By next month the only place you'll be able to find my name is in a medical journal."

Marsha averted her eyes while she lit a cigarette. Her concentration on the simple act made Nancy uncomfortable. She realized that once they had disposed of her health, they had little to talk about.

"Let me give Matt a call. He'd be furious if he knew you were here and didn't see him."

"Marsha, I want to know what I've got to do to get my job back."

Marsha put down the receiver. Her smile melted away. "There's no way I can put you in front of a camera. You understand that, don't you?"

"But—"

"It's my decision. Matt and I have discussed it, and he agrees with me, but it's my decision. You're too hot. Nan, you've been brought back from the dead. You'll be a center of controversy until cryonics becomes commonplace." Marsha sagged forward in her chair. Her austere executive veneer had crumbled. "I wish there was something I could do."

A lump rose in Nancy's throat. For a moment she could barely speak. Then she saw a ray of hope. *Until it becomes commonplace.* She ran the phrase over in her mind. It's what I expected all along, she realized. "The only controversy surrounding me is being created by ignorant, prejudiced people. If I have to educate them before I can report the news, well, that's just another bridge to cross," she said firmly.

"Good!" Marsha clapped her hand down on the desk. "No more shrinking violet. The role didn't fit you anyway. If you've got the guts to make cryonics a household word, I'll bump heads with the big guys upstairs until we get you back on the air."

Nancy knew just where to start. She reached for Marsha's telephone and dialed NAC headquarters. The conversation took only a moment.

". . . I'll have a car downstairs in fifteen minutes."

"Thank you, Dr. Stepp," Nancy answered and hung up.

"Everything okay?" Marsha asked.

Nancy shot her a wide smile from the doorway. "From now on you'd better assign a reporter to cover me."

Nancy reached the sidewalk just as the black limousine pulled up in front of the building. She headed right for it.

There was no mistaking the NAC-1 license plate. Dr. Stepp's shining pate popped out of the rear window.

"Nancy, your call came at a most opportune time," Stepp said buoyantly. The driver ran around to open the door. Stepp slid back into the far corner of the salon-sized rear seat as Nancy got in.

"I didn't expect you to come yourself, Doctor."

"It was a stroke of luck that you called when you did. I was just on my way out."

"I didn't want you to disrupt your day."

"Not a bit of it, Nancy. Besides, I've got a notion of why you called. You've got too much spunk to let yourself get pushed around for very long. I've licked the scientific problem of cryonic suspension, but there's a lot more to it. There's the atavistic fear of the unknown. The cold sting of death that makes people turn away from you. I expected it. Isn't it about time someone shone a light under the bushel?"

All at once the distance of Nancy's friends, their awkward silences and fish-eyed glances, came into clear perspective. She found it almost a relief to know she hadn't been dreaming it.

"Doctor," Nancy whispered, "I want to fight back. I want people to know that cryonics really works."

"That's good, because we're on our way into round one. You can stand up at our stockholders' meeting. Show the world that you're the same person you always were. Millions of people who know they're dying and live in fear and misery will draw hope from you."

"What can I say?" Nancy asked excitedly.

"Just tell the truth. Bear witness to your own experiences in your own words. I must tell you that Victor opposes the idea. He wouldn't even broach the subject with you. He told me that you were still too weak. Tell me, Nancy, are you too weak?"

Nancy heard the hint of a childish dare in the doctor's soft voice. She knew there was more to it. The New York Stock Exchange had halted trading in NAC stock until the buyers could catch up to the market.

"Aside from your kindly interest, Doctor, I daresay that having me speak might be very good for the cryonics business."

"It might be," Stepp answered with a smile. "If so, we

deserve it. We've made a remarkable contribution to medical
science. The most unethical thing we could do would be to
keep it a secret."

"I think you're right," Nancy said. She also realized that
she liked being needed.

Willie Garvin sipped his third cup of coffee. The coffee
shop's plate-glass window afforded a perfect view of the side
entrance to North American Chemicals' New York headquarters. He had picked out the spot two weeks before.

Suddenly he jumped from his stool. The black limousine
had stopped for a red light at the end of the block. He
slapped a five-dollar bill down on the counter and darted out
into the street. A burst of panic shot through his stomach.
There was no place to hide. The crowd of newsmen had gone
inside, leaving only a skeleton crew behind, and a few
pedestrians who paused to watch them. He spun around to face
the building wall, like a man blinded by the sunlight, just as
Nancy Seymour emerged from the limousine. For a moment
he thought he could smell her fragrance across the twenty
yards that separated them. Then he hunched his shoulders
and scurried away.

Nancy's eyes fixed on the tweed jacket until it was a small
speck rounding the corner. Stepp and the stockholders' meeting receded from her mind. All at once her feet had a will of
their own. She found herself halfway down the block before
Stepp caught up with her.

"Nancy, you walked past the door. It's back that way," he
said with a quizzical frown.

She stared at him blankly for a moment until his words began to make sense.

"Is anything wrong?" he asked quickly.

"Wrong?" Nancy repeated in a voice so low that he had to
cock his head to hear her. "No . . . I just thought I saw
someone I know."

13

A standing-room crowd packed the brightly lit auditorium. They were all well attired and decently polite, the way Nancy imagined stockholders would be. But she could feel their eyes scrutinizing her like the fine print on a mortgage. The balcony bristled television cameras, and a trapeze of microphones hung down over the podium. Nancy realized that her presence had been anticipated. Stepp held her back in the wings until the auditorium was darkened for a slide presentation. Then they walked out to the stage to take the two empty seats at the speakers' table. When the lights came on, the audience gasped discreetly and began to smile. For a moment Nancy thought they would applaud. Profits shooting off the bar charts had put everybody in a very good mood.

Arch Kholer completed his opening remarks. Then he turned toward Nancy and Stepp. For an instant his eyes flashed the relief of a magician who finds that his rabbit really is waiting inside the hat. He beamed confidence.

"Ladies and gentlemen," he announced, "Nancy Seymour has graciously consented to join us for the discussion of NAC's newly formed subsidiary, Cryonics Marketing, Inc. But first, Dr. A. A. Stepp will introduce this remarkable process."

Stepp laid a reassuring hand on Nancy's shoulder as he got to his feet. "Look how happy you've made everyone," he whispered. "This will be a snap for you. Just act like you're on television."

Suddenly Nancy was back in her element. She smiled into the lights, radiating self-assurance. Stepp took the podium, but she knew the cameras were on her. The press releases stacked on the table caught her eye. She read the banner and realized what they had missed by coming in late.

NAC STOCK UP 126% ON THE STRENGTH OF CRYONICS BREAKTHROUGH. OVERALL CORPORATE PROFITS EXPECTED TO DOUBLE BY YEAR END.

This is more like a victory party, Nancy thought. Stepp should have had me pop out of a cake. As she watched the audience's eyes widen, she, too, began to listen to Stepp's presentation.

". . . We have revolutionized the practice of medicine. The fear of death has become obsolete. As of today, your company has begun accepting deposits for cryonic suspension. Our only limit will be our ability to produce 'life-support tanks' and the training of technicians to operate our sophisticated equipment. We shall be well along by year end. Our cryonic process is being scrutinized by the scientific community and the inevitable agencies of the federal government. We welcome it. They will verify our major scientific breakthroughs. Once a subject is certified dead, we can have the body immersed in cryonic suspension within six minutes. This high level of efficiency assures no further organ deterioration will occur so long as oxygen is fed to the brain. Our vacuum suction pump has solved the time-consuming problem of draining out the bodies' natural fluids so they will not expand to cause cell damage during the freezing process. . . ."

Nancy's hand wandered to the small scar just below her navel. She cringed at the thought of her blood being pumped out of her body. She could picture the humming machine sucking her dry as a cocoon.

". . . and based upon our well-documented success with Nancy Seymour"—Stepp gestured broadly at Nancy—"I predict that this antiquated law will be changed. People will not have to be certified dead to receive cryonic suspension.

Cryonics is safe and will be regarded as just another scientific procedure while a cure for a terminal disease is being developed. Yes, I predict that cryonic suspension will be available to the general public within two years. Conservatively estimating our capacity, and with an initial deposit priced at only five thousand dollars, your company estimates first-year revenues from CMI at two and one half billion dollars."

The stockholders rose to their feet, applauding until Stepp reluctantly raised his hands for quiet. Kholer strode across the stage to embrace him, and the applause grew still louder. Nancy's mind wandered. Profit . . . profit . . . profit; she began counting the number of times she heard the word.

"Well, Nancy, I guess you should take that one yourself."

"What?" She realized Stepp was speaking to her. He had begun accepting questions from the audience.

"Nancy . . ." She picked out the questioner in the second row. It was Bob Newsome of ABC.

"Hi, Bob."

The young newsman's features remained sternly professional. "Nancy, as a former journalist, how do you feel about being a shill for this immortality dream?"

The audience gasped, but to Nancy the question seemed legitimate enough. She would have asked it herself if she were standing in his place.

"Bob, you can't ignore death. It won't go away just because you refuse to face it. NAC has done something wonderful. Everyone has a right to share it." She watched the audience's eyes. She could tell they were rooting for her. The applause began to roll in the moment she had finished.

Nancy arrived home in a flush of excitement. Her brain was swimming. She had never imagined that so much money could be made on cryonics. And I'll bet you don't know the half of it, she told herself. At first the idea struck her as obscene. She pictured lines of desperate people thrusting money at Cryonics Marketing, Inc. She knew that she had just been the first of many. Her anger melted into confusion. There was a colder light. Business as usual, she thought. NAC saved your life. Now they'll make a bundle. It was no worse than many things she could think of.

Her hands began to shake. All at once she couldn't bear the idea of being alone. She started toward her bedroom. A bolt of pain shot up her leg as her knee slammed into the corner of an end table that shouldn't have been there.

"Damn you, John," she shouted out loud with more venom than she knew she possessed.

The outburst shocked her. She ran into her bedroom. But it wasn't hers. It was a place that belonged in *House Beautiful*. She could have been in a hotel room. Her address book was still in the top left desk drawer. She riffled from page to page. The names seemed blurry and indistinct. She sensed that any call would just be an imposition. She hadn't the strength for the polite answers people give when they're only half-listening. She started back at the front of the book, this time almost in a frenzy.

Then she made herself stop. Owen Bundy's name lay right over her fingertip. He's my doctor, she thought, swallowing her pride. He'll have to see me. Her hands were shaking as she punched his number.

"Owen." She started in a tone of strident anger. "You haven't called in weeks. Don't you give a damn about me anymore?" Nancy caught her breath. It was not what she had wanted to say. None of it. There was a dead silence at the other end of the line. "Owen, I'm sorry. I don't know what's got into me. I'm . . ."

"Nancy, what's the trouble, child?"

"I don't know. I'm so confused."

"Are you at home? I'll come right over."

"Yes . . . No. Let me come to your office. Please."

"All right," Bundy said softly.

The old man slowly swiveled his chair to face his bookshelves. The cracked leather tomes that held the world's small knowledge of military fever were arrayed at convenient eye level. The first thought to pop into Owen Bundy's mind filled him with sadness: The cure did not take.

14

"I've got a nasty hunch that the process might be reversing itself," Amos Stepp said solemnly. He leaned over his desk and wagged a chubby finger at John Victor. "I'm not positive, mind you, but we can't ignore the possibility."

Victor could feel the beginning of a tic under his eye. He wished he understood more about the "process." He had tried, but Stepp's pedantic manner irritated him like a stone in his shoe.

"Damned late in the day to find out, Amos," he said. "When the hell will we know for sure?"

Stepp shrugged. "Maybe never. These mood swings might not be physical at all. This is all new to us, John. Who knows how much her subconscious recalls of her experiences? I had hoped the new furniture, new clothes, and all would inhibit any reactive memories. But I'll tell you this much: I spent two hours with her today and she is nowhere near her original psychological profile. Now, we both knew this might happen."

"Are you suggesting she should see a psychiatrist?" Victor blurted out. He was amazed that Stepp had taken the interest to notice. He could have added a thing or two, but thought better of it. He could see no benefit to having Amos Stepp

71

meddle in his personal life. Nancy was not sleeping. What would Stepp make of that? he wondered. He could hear her padding around in the middle of the night. Then she would catapult from bursts of energy and enthusiasm into fits of lethargy and depression. One moment she would be the gregarious, friendly person her television audience recalled, only to withdraw into reclusive hostility. His mind flashed to a long list of drugs. Sure, there was a desired, optimal effect. But Stepp was certainly right about one thing. They had no idea what the cumulative side effects might be, or where they might lead. Victor felt like a halfback who had fought his way over the goal line, only to be told he had to run back down the field.

"No, of course we don't want her seeing a psychiatrist. But I don't want her going to pieces in public, either. Step up her dosages of lithium. Use vitamin capsules to disguise them. Worst comes to worst, we'll just have to ease her out of the marketing campaign. It'll hurt, especially now. But in the long run we'll get just as rich, a little slower." Stepp rubbed his pink chin. "Damned thing is, John, she seemed to enjoy it. She got up cold at that stockholders' meeting and really handled herself. Well, maybe I'm imagining the whole thing. Maybe this nervousness and alienation are just a passing result of all the hoopla. Still, I think you should be a most attentive husband."

"Easier said than done." Victor answered with a scowl. "We're not very close, you know. Amos, I hate to admit this, but she won't even let me touch her. That's not exactly great for my ego."

"To hell with your ego." Stepp exploded. "I said attentive, not lecherous. She had a terrible experience. Don't lay a hand on her if you think it will cause the slightest anxiety. Perhaps you think I shouldn't have said that?"

"No, Amos, you know best." Victor was just as glad to drop the subject. It hurt his pride to admit that he had not slept with his wife for the year preceding her illness. But Stepp's remark about her "terrible experience" lingered painfully. He would never forget the look in her eyes when she awoke from her nightmare.

"John, can you arrange for Nancy to be here tomorrow morning? I'd like to give her a complete examination. I think it's best that we hold the public appearances for a while. News stories about her should be able to keep up interest."

Victor got to his feet. "I'll need some cash, Amos," he said casually. "A few small debts to settle, and I'd rather not sell stock. A fifty-thousand advance ought to see me through."

"All right, John," Stepp said after a moment. "I guess we can afford it. Pick up the money tomorrow when you stop by with Nancy."

The phone rang. Stepp shot it a nasty glare, and Victor could have sworn he saw the white plastic box cringe. Finally Stepp pressed a button on the console of controls built into his armchair.

"I told you I wasn't to be interrupted, Maude," he said with an icy calm.

"It's a Dr. Owen Bundy. He insisted it was urgent."

Victor's eyes widened. He choked back a gasp of surprise. "He was Nancy's—"

"I know very well," Stepp mused.

"What the devil can he want?"

Stepp pressed a chubby finger to his lips and turned back to the phone. "Yes, Dr. Bundy," he said most cordially. "How can I help you?"

"I've just spoken with Nancy Seymour. She sounded almost irrational . . . frantic. I'll need detailed information on your treatment for her military fever before I can work with her."

"She's been under a great deal of strain, you know," Stepp said calmly. "Might be nothing at all to worry about. The child has been through so much. We wouldn't want to make more of it than it is, would we?"

"Dr. Stepp, I can assure you that I am very sympathetic to Nancy's condition," Bundy responded firmly. He had been around doctors too long to let Stepp's oily manner put him off the track. Researchers were all the same, Bundy thought. Their darkest fear was exposing their work to someone who might steal the grand idea for himself. And that included everybody. He continued in a careful, measured tone, "Please bear in mind, Doctor, that diminished capacity is a recognized tertiary symptom of military fever. We can't ignore any possibility, however remote."

"Are you suggesting that our cure might not have held?" To Victor's surprise, Stepp's response was quietly humble.

There was just the hint of a tremor in his voice as he leaned closer to the speaker phone.

Victor sidled up behind him. "Tell the nosy bastard to go to hell," he whispered into Stepp's ear. Stepp's lips curled into a snarl that sent Victor retreating back to his chair.

"Nothing, Dr. Bundy. I was just shuffling some papers," he said quickly. "Please go on."

"You've never fully published your findings. I don't know where to begin. I've no idea what strain of antibody you might have found effective, nor the culture medium or incubation period. Nothing. What work I've seen appears to have treated the cure almost as an afterthought. I understand that the cryonic process was your main concern, but I've got a patient to look after. Dr. Stepp, we may just require some simple remedial medication to address a minor side effect, but I certainly do not want to be tinkering in the dark. So if you would be good enough to promptly provide me with your course of treatment . . ."

"Frankly, Dr. Bundy, we're still not ready to publish. Some questions remain. I know you were very close to Nancy. It's natural she should call you. Let me assure you that we'll be happy to open our files to you. NAC will cooperate in every way possible. After all, the patient comes first."

"I'm delighted to hear that, Dr. Stepp. Nancy's due here shortly. I'll give her a thorough physical and get back to you."

"Please do. We share your concern."

Victor could barely wait for the connection to click dead. He had the feeling that his stomach had sunk through the floor. "Amos, you've lost your marbles. I don't want that righteous old man poking over Nancy."

But Stepp had other ideas. Events unfolded before his eyes. Moves and countermoves. Suddenly there was a great deal of money at stake. More then he had ever expected. NAC stock was selling like a share in eternity. The accounting department was inundated daily with sacks of mail filled with unsolicited bids for suspension. The boys in the mail room nearly keeled over at the sight of all that cash. Yes, cash. They began fighting over the thickest envelopes. First guards were hired. They sat on high stools and watched everybody like a pack of chicken hawks. But the volume of cash was staggering. One morning it reached a hundred pounds. Then the entire mail-room operation was moved to the largest vault in Weston, Connecticut. Now Stepp reveled in his own emerging-star status. That was one perk he hadn't expected. So perhaps there'll be other twists, he thought. Money brings out the hyena in man's nature. If poor Nancy's ill, she should be tended. So long as the integrity of the cryonic process is preserved. Let her quietly fade away, and a sizable problem would fade with her. Ever so reluctantly he allowed as how Nancy might have been his second miscalculation. But at least he could be sure of her husband. He always liked a man with hungry eyes. They made the best partners.

"Well, you never know, John. This Bundy might be quite a competent chap," he answered carefully, deliberately distorting the thrust of Victor's outrage. "We should at least go over and have a chat with him. We owe Nancy that much."

Nancy abandoned her taxi two blocks short of Owen Bundy's town house. There had been a glint in the driver's eyes. He spent far too much time checking the rearview mirror. His look made her uncomfortable. She stalled in front of a store window until she was sure he had turned the corner. "Nasty, leering man," she caught herself thinking aloud. There had been a string of them recently, she realized. Men whose look was almost an assault. She wondered if her isolation had made her sensitive. She used to be able to look them in the eye and stare them into an embarrassed blink.

She walked with purposeful speed, weaving through the crowded sidewalk like a driver on an obstacle course. Bundy's compact little building was nestled between two high-rises on the next block. She fixed her eyes on it and stared until the tired red bricks seemed to glow. Being dwarfed among the giants made no difference. It stood out with weathered dignity like a safe cove on a stormy night.

Nancy struggled to get a grip on herself. She knew she had taken nothing stronger than vitamins since leaving the hospital. It certainly wasn't drugs. Then why not madness? How Victorian that sounds, she thought. There was no denying that the faces around her pulsed with hostility. She hurried for Bundy's doorway. God knows, she thought, a trip back from the dead would be enough to unhinge a block of stone. Then she was inside and her heartbeat slowed.

The faded wallpaper and tired green carpet conjured up a

better past. A new receptionist in a crisp white uniform smiled across the room. "Go right in, Miss Seymour. The doctor is expecting you."

Then she got up and opened the door for Nancy. Nancy knew it was a simple act of courtesy, but she still found it bleakly depressing that a girl of approximately her own age should think her so incapacitated.

Bundy rose to meet her. The sparkle in his eyes was a warm beacon and she spread her arms wide. But it took only a moment to realize that they weren't alone. A shape stirred behind a high-backed chair. Nancy's stomach jumped. Stepp's gleaming pate rose into view like the top of a soft-coned rocket. His smile was a red flag to Nancy's anger. In an instant Bundy realized his mistake. By then it was far too late.

"You," Nancy sputtered, pointing an accusing finger at her old friend. "I trusted you, Dr. Bundy. If I'd wanted to see Dr. Stepp, I'd have called him."

"Nancy, I did what I thought best," he answered defensively. "The military fever——"

"I trusted you," she said curtly. "He doesn't give a damn about me. He's just using me to hype his damned stock. But I thought you cared. I trusted you."

Nancy spun around, leaving Bundy standing slack-jawed in the center of his office. Her square shoulders and rapid gait masked the sting of betrayal rising from deep within her.

Her feet seemed to have a will of their own. She found herself walking quickly with no clear destination in mind. But soon the route grew familiar. She was nearing Rockefeller Center. A picture of the newsroom flashed through her brain. There was no joy in it, and she forced the image aside. Instead she concentrated on the dozens of airline offices packed into ten blocks of Fifth Avenue. Only the names atop the plate-glass windows were different. The promise they held was always the same. Escape. Where? Nancy wondered almost frantically. It didn't really matter. Anyplace far away where her face wasn't a beacon for gawkers. Where she could have some time for herself.

The sky opened up with a great crash of thunder. Black clouds raced across the sun, and in a moment the streets became dark and somber as twilight. Bill Addison barely noticed. Then the large, sluggish raindrops began to pelt down. They splattered down with an intensity that sent the midday crowds scurrying for doorways. Addison never broke stride. He wanted to put miles between himself and NBC.

Their answers had stunned him. He wasn't used to finding himself speechless, standing slack-jawed before the minions of bureaucracy. Yet that was just what he had done. First came the glances of hostile caution every time he mentioned Nancy's name. A full five minutes of haggling to convince the wispy thin, bespectacled woman that he wasn't a spy from a rival network, or some such nonsense. They both knew it was a stall. She was waiting for a higher-class flunky to get her off the hook. A fat man in a pinstripe suit joined the woman. They acted as though Nancy Seymour were a poor and distant relation. A distinct embarrassment to the firm. Yes, they would leave word of his call. No, they certainly didn't expect to see her. No, they did not know how she could be reached and they absolutely could not give out an address or telephone number. The angrier Addison grew, the more information he demanded, asking questions for which he had long since memorized the answers. He knew that a visit to the station was no more than a convenient long shot. A remotely possible route around NAC's tight ring of security that, if it worked out, might have spared Nancy some embarrassment. He was not particularly surprised by their rebuff. Only by the depth of the reaction he received. Their stone facade never swayed. That was the part that left him shaking his head. It wasn't . . . He fumbled for the word. Decent.

Thunder quaked through the concrete, rattling plate-glass windows and sending a shiver down his spine. The rain pelted into puddles. He looked straight across Fifth Avenue. Even the traffic seemed to have melted away in the storm. Then his heart stopped and he froze dead in his tracks.

"Nancy." He shouted across the empty expanse that should have been packed with midday humanity. For a moment she didn't hear, and like any good New Yorker maintained her purposeful stride. It a moment she would be lost. He shouted again. She wiped the rain out of her eyes and turned tentatively toward the sound of his voice. Addison couldn't wait. He bolted across the broad avenue, oblivious of puddles and horns and the sound of screeching brakes, never taking his eyes off her face lest she vanish back into the grayness that surrounded her. Suddenly the time between them evaporated with the distance he crossed. He felt her body trembling in his arms, shaking, wet, and pulsing energy. He never wanted to let go. A broad grin slowly spread across his face.

He whispered in her ear, "Let's get in out of the rain."

He could feel her breathing through his raincoat. She squeezed his arm hard, just as he had done to her. They were both real.

"Your place or mine?" she answered once she was convinced that he wasn't part of a dream.

15

Nancy watched the trees that framed the country road in a canopy of greens. The air carried a soft chill, clearing her head like a morning shower. She had forgotten how much she enjoyed leaving New York's oppressive heat. She could see it rippling off the concrete streets and that made the country seem even fresher. Maybe distance can solve problems, she thought, or at least give them some time to solve themselves. She scanned the road and the rolling hills beyond. Finally, saving the best for last, she watched Bill, who divided his attention between the road and her.

"You're feeling better," he said with some relief and a good deal of satisfaction. "It was just a matter of hustling you out of the clutches of all those damned doctors."

"I'm NAC's prize patient. What a prize. I can just picture Dr. Stepp and my devoted husband wringing their hands while they watched me thaw out. If I didn't defrost alive, I think Arch Kholer would have had them frozen. I suppose this was John's big break. I can't really blame them for going into a dead faint every time I cough. They've got big bucks riding on my freshly preserved body."

"To hell with them," Bill snapped. He didn't see the humor

in their greedy concern. "They're using you, and you know it. Why do you stand for it?"

"Sure they're using me. And I used them to save my life. Don't you think I owe them a little something?" Nancy answered philosophically. "Besides, it won't last much longer. They've got customers lined up around the block. People are fighting to get themselves frozen. I'm only a hot item until the next dummy's thawed out for a miracle cure. Jesus, nobody's ever heard of military fever. Wait till they do their thing on cancer or one of the other biggies. Lickety-split and I'm yesterday's news. Just sit tight, sweetheart."

Addison wasn't so patient. A roller coaster of emotions flashed through his brain with a jolt that made his temples ache. Nancy had died. He still carried the pain of it even as he felt her next to him. He had seen no hope in cryonic suspension. Her life had been over. Everything he knew, or believed, had told him that a dead person was dead. Such things couldn't be changed. For the first time in his life, he had been lonely. Once he even phoned John Victor, but nobody answered. Later he was glad. He dug up assignments as far away from New York as possible. Being in Japan helped a little. There was less to remind him of their past together.

Work kept him busy. He was hired to plan security for a proposed airport that would blacktop over two thousand acres of farmland north of Osaka. The government was digging in for a repitition of the Tokyo airport riots. It was a long-term project, and once under way took his time on only an irregular basis. Mostly he traveled and thought about Nancy.

The news of her awakening reached him like a bolt of fantasy from a television screen. Up to the very minute it happened, he had never considered it even remotely possible. He still wasn't sure. To see Nancy alive again was a miracle. That much he knew. But miracles did not alter the general truth. My will-o'-the-wisp, he thought. I've got you now. I found you in a storm and I claim you against all the world. I've no more patience left, only love. He had a strong sense that good fortune was a fleeting thing. He didn't want to waste a minute of their present.

The desk clerk looked up from his newspaper at the sound of feet padding across the deep pile carpet. Nancy found his movements pleasing and very appropriate to the lugubrious mahogany fortress of cubbyholes and brass keys that surrounded him. The guest register was a tome bound in green leather that he swiveled to meet their approach. All the names had been penned with great flourish, in real india ink, as though the guests were competing in a contest. No ballpoints at the Red Lion Inn. Nancy was convinced the clerk would slap Bill's hand had he the temerity to turn a page back for a peek at who might have come before. It was that kind of place.

The clerk sized them up and carefully selected one of the heavy, shiny keys. Then he paused and furrowed his deeply tanned brow.

"Is your luggage in the car, Mr. . . . Addison?" he asked with some politeness.

Nancy felt a flush of embarrassment spread across her cheeks. Suddenly she began to laugh.

"We left New York in kind of a hurry," Bill said sheepishly. Nancy noticed the brightly dressed matrons on their way to the porch for a sunset pink gin. Occasionally one would pause to check out the new clientele. Then her distinguished escort would give her a little tug on the elbow and they would be back on course, heading out into the warm evening. The wide screen door let in the soft sounds of birds and of an orchestra playing in the town square a block away. They went well together, she thought. She knew, without ever having been to Stockbridge that there would be at least one whitewashed church with a tall steeple and bell tower and a bronzed cannon in front of the town hall. Suddenly she wanted very much to stay.

"We'll buy whatever we need," she said to the startled desk clerk. "Now please register us. Then point us to the best restaurant in town. I'm starved."

The elm-lined street was shuttered and dark. But the silence had none of that tense electricity of the big city that made you walk warily, wanting to glance back at the sound of footsteps. Instead, the pleasant absence of traffic and human noise allowed the quieter sounds of birds and crickets to be heard. Nancy paused to listen, as though for the first time. The sounds made her happy. She had the feeling of stumbling on a remarkable new sensory thrill. She tugged Bill's arm so he would listen too.

"It's beautiful," she whispered so as not to disturb the darkness. "Why didn't you find me sooner?"

Addison knew her question was mostly in jest, but it brought a pang of guilt all the same. It was certainly not that she had ever been far from his thoughts.

"Stupid pride, I suppose," he confessed. "Every time I saw you on television, and God knows you were on like a beer commercial, you seemed so wrapped up in the cryonics thing. There were always so many people hovering around you. I just felt I'd . . ."

"Be in the way? You jerk." Nancy smiled. "That was their idea, not mine. You should have known that I never really cared about any of it. Now my days as a left-handed celebrity are almost over. I've got more important plans."

She quickened her pace. Their hotel porch lights shone like a beacon a block ahead. The swings and wicker benches had long since emptied, and she noticed that a bright red carpet ran down the four steps, right to the sidewalk.

Nancy knew Addison was waiting, perhaps growing impatient. She took a short, nervous puff of her cigarette. The unaccustomed acrid bite of smoke almost started her coughing. She could hear her heart pounding through the thin silk robe wrapped tightly around her. You've brushed your hair for fifteen minutes, she thought angrily. What the hell can you do next? She stared at her reflection in the glaring light of the bathroom mirror. When she held her breath, she could hear the faint sound of the breeze rustling the leaves beside her window. Or is it the rustling of bed sheets? she thought in a burst of panic. Her skin was clammy white and she felt the dampness of perspiration that made the silk cling to her body. You're scared shitless, she realized. You're frozen tight.

The truth stunned her like a slap in the face. Avoiding John was one thing, she thought; that had been easy in the best of times. But Bill . . . Why now? She pictured his body, slim and hard, the way she had always liked men to feel. But the thought only brought a coldness to her stomach that she couldn't explain. She slung open the bathroom door and stared into the darkened bedroom.

"Bill, please turn on the light," she said in a voice barely under control. "We've got to talk."

Bill Addison listened. He sat up and leaned forward so he could watch Nancy's eyes while she spoke. She never advanced to closer than ten feet, but even at that distance it was perfectly clear to him that she was on the verge of going off like a fragmentation bomb. Finally she ceased her pacing and took the chair farthest from the bed, where she immediately began to fidget nervously with the hem of her robe. Addison was certain that she would have preferred the conversation be held by long-distance phone.

"I just don't understand," he said, finally baring his frustration. "Is it something I've done?" He knew it was the wrong question even as the words passed his lips.

Nancy shook her head sadly. "God, no. Bill, you're the best thing that's ever happened to me. I know I'm making a fool of myself. All I know is that I don't want anyone, not even you, to touch me. Of course you don't understand. I must sound insane. I don't understand myself. I feel terrible about it. You can see that. I'm being torn apart. Jesus, part of me wants you like crazy. But I can't. I just can't."

"Do you want me to leave?"

"No!" Nancy shot back. "Don't leave me alone." Then the tension drained out of her body and she sank down in her chair. Addison saw glistening tears forming on her cheeks. He stepped behind her and laid his hands gently on her shoulders.

"You can go to sleep now," he whispered. "I'll be here."

He watched her force herself back together. She did it with deep breaths. Gradually the muscles around her shoulders began to loosen. Her eyes were averted downward while she crossed to the bathroom. When she came out, her movements were lighter, less troubled. Addison wondered what she might have taken.

"Are you feeling better?" he asked.

"Yes, a little. Bill, I so want you to understand that I really care for you. Don't be angry. Please. We'll talk about it in the morning. I just don't feel up to it right now." Her voice grew drowsy.

Is this part of the "process"? Addison wondered. Some kinky little side effect that nobody thought about? They can bring you out of the deep freeze. But no more sex. Some hormone thaws a little too slowly. Herr Doktor, next time vee turn der screw left and get a topless dancer. Addison rubbed his eyes. They still have a lot to learn, the boys at NAC. Why should they give a shit? They're rolling in money. Stockholders and banks come first, he thought with disgusted resignation. Thaw 'em out and get them walking. The big bucks are in turnover. He sat very still for a long while after he was sure Nancy was asleep. No more damned tinkering doctors, he thought. Then it'll work out, in time.

Nancy looked straight up through the mist at the dangling light bulb. It was very bright and for a moment she thought it might be the sun. Everything around it was black. She squinted and turned her head slightly. The bed beneath her back was hard and sticky with moisture. She vaguely wanted to shift her weight but sensed that the effort would be in vain. Her body felt heavy as stone. A flash of misery choked her throat. It passed as quickly as it had come. Then she felt nothing, again. Not even bored. The light began to fade.

Soon, her inner clock told her. Soon now you'll soar. It was not a memory, only a sense of what would come. Things flowed in a pattern. The light, the hardness, the soaring. The colors behind her eyes began to change. A quivering sensation crept through her body. It was like an alarm going off. The pattern had changed. The sweet music in her head turned to static. She felt the ground shake. It was wrong. She wanted to soar. Wanted . . . ? Instead, she recognized the nibblings of fear, like an old recollection shut up in the attic. Something without a name. She was cold all over. A great shadow spread out to block the light. It swooped down. Flee, her body screamed. The shadow choked off escape like a hot, wet blanket. Breath came in one sharp searing pain. Its wings churned to a fury of black chaos. Then it entered her and the blackness shattered like broken glass. She tumbled, flaying in panic at the leaden blanket. Suddenly it was still, and very hot.

"Willie!" she screamed aloud.

Addison sat bolt upright at the edge of his chair. Nancy

leaped to her feet. She held a trembling hand in front of her face. Tears poured down her cheeks.

"Willie!" she screamed again before Addison could shake her fully awake.

16

The hotel room fronted Eighth Avenue. It was a small, dirty place that conjured up gag lines about hunchbacked rats and suitcases left in the hallway. Willie Garvin knew all the best ones came from one Marx Brothers movie and he leafed through his card-file memory for the title. Play some word games, pick out names for the cockroaches, kill time. He had decided hours before that anything was easier than trying to sleep over the glare of neon lights that no flimsy shade could keep out. The racket of trucks and angry taxi horns wafted up with the smell of ripe garbage. It comes with the sleaze, Willie thought. All one price. When you get sick enough, you'll leave. No I won't. He mentally stiffened his backbone. You know what you have to do.

The rap on the door sent a shudder through his body.

"Who is it?" he asked timidly, slipping on his pants as he spoke.

"Max's Liquor."

"I called an hour ago. Where've you been?" Willie said with more relief than anger.

"I'm here now, pal. So how's about openin' the door so I can go the hell home."

Willie carefully turned the bolt, leaving the chain in place so he could peek out without surrendering his meager security. A tall, skinny kid glared at him from the dimness of the corridor.

"Well, slide it in," Willie demanded.

The kid pursed his lips in disgust. He had tried this trick before and knew it wouldn't work. Still, he went through the motions of twisting the paper bag against the door frame. Every time he turned his head, Willie could see the shadows cast into the acne pits that covered his face.

"It don't fit," the kid announced triumphantly. His lips curled into a nasty smirk. "Come on, buddy, if you want yer booze, open the damned door. I ain't gonna rape you."

Willie felt his heart jump. His palms were clammy as he fumbled with the chain. A flash of panic froze his hand. What if he's the one? Maybe they know. . . But the dryness in his throat gave him courage and he slid the bolt free. The kid kept the bottle tucked under his arm like a football. His gaze went straight over Willie's head to the litter of newspapers that covered the floor like a second carpet. Only reluctantly did he slide the bottle forward. His other palm was held open. "That'll be nine-twenty-five."

Willie fished a bill out of his pocket. It was a single. He knew better than to flash his entire roll, so he fished again. This time he landed a ten and thrust both bills at the kid, grabbing his bottle at the same time. The kid took the tip without comment.

"You like to read, eh, buddy? What else you like to do?" he said without changing his smirk.

"That'll be all," Willie answered. He knew it sounded stupid. The sort of phrase he would use in a good restaurant, not a rat-hole dive where decent manners mark you for a tourist. He shifted his weight nervously, waiting for the kid to count his money and leave.

The kid ignored him. He sauntered to the center of the room, lightly kicking newspapers as he went. Willie had a sudden urge to dash into the hall. Even in simpler times he had possessed a nose for danger—a weak man's instinct for survival, he'd call it. He turned back and shot a glance at the kid. Long, dirty blond hair covered his thick neck and sinuous shoulders. For a moment he was tempted to forget his danger and his mission.

"I said that'll be all." Willie managed a scowl.

"Okay, forget it. I thought you might be a lonely gentle-man instead of a cheap bastard. I thought you might like to share a drink. But I see you don't. That's okay with me too."

The kid tilted a practiced eye around the room, making it clear to Willie that he might just have more on his mind than a simple drink. But there wasn't so much as a pack of ciga-rettes on the bureau and only Willie's rumpled suit draped over the back of a chair. Slim pickings all around. Willie inched halfway out into the hall. A scream of panic was deli-cately balanced at the edge of his lips. The kid shook off any notion of an easy mark. He crossed the room in two strides, brushing Willie aside as he took off down the dim corridor.

"Faggot creep," he shouted so everybody on the floor could hear through the paper-thin walls. Willie slammed the door and bolted it locked. His hands were shaking.

"It isn't worth it," he said aloud. Look at yourself. You jump at the first punk who comes along. He could feel the tears on his cheeks and the lump in his throat as he wrestled the cap off the bottle. He filled the dirty gray water glass with vodka, but needed both hands to gulp it down.

In a moment the warmth began to spread through his body. His jaw slackened as he slumped into the tattered arm-chair. In his haste the vodka had dripped down the front of his shirt and onto his trousers. He didn't notice until the dam-age was done. "Look at yourself," he whispered sadly. Willie Garvin, you're forty-four years old and just not cut out for heroism. Forget this madness and go home while you still can. Another long sip and his mind drifted to the pure white beach and blue waters off Key West. He would sit for hours and watch the swordfish jump. Go home, you damned fool. Nobody expects anything of you anyway. Then his eyes drifted to the week's accumulation of newspapers and maga-zines that covered the seedy carpet. He wasn't used to a mess and would never have tolerated it in his own prim little cabin. But here it seemed proper. Even right. The newspapers were as alien to him as their random resting places. *The Wall Street Journal, Barron's, Value Line, Dun's Review.* He tilted his slightly tipsy head to make out the names of a few more. They were all equally unfamiliar. Their information, coded into small, arcane symbols, had to be dragged out with a magnifying glass and dictionary. Reading them gave him a headache and made him grind his teeth in frustration. Still, he knew he was missing a lot, slogging like a clod through a field of daisies.

Willie had thought about calling his friend Barry, the stockbroker. Barry would understand. He could whiz through all that Wall Street gibberish like shit through a goose. It was very tempting. But that would be another risk. It was far better that nobody knew he was in New York. He wasn't supposed to be here, not ever. No point taking stupid chances, he had decided at last. Besides, he was pretty sure that it would not take a financial genius to get the message. North American Chemicals was the hottest stock on the Street. The thought made him boil with anger. He poured another quick drink in an effort to sort out the love from the hatred that turned his knuckles white as he squeezed the glass. After a moment's effort he gave up. It didn't really matter. He knew what he had to do. A man doesn't often get a second chance, he decided. I can have it both ways. Do what's right, and get my fair share, all at the same time.

They had exchanged hardly a word during the three-hour drive. After a while the silence grew to be a heavy blanket drawn around them. Just the thought of phrasing words became a labor. Nancy considered how much longer an unpleasant drive seemed to take. She thought she owed an explanation, but somehow it didn't seem important. More like a duty than something she really wanted to do. It brought to mind a bad date, after the boy had gone too far and everybody was embarrassed. So she stared at the road and pretended to be interested in the green rolling hills that had made her so happy just the day before.

When she thought about it, she could not decide whether it had been her frigidity or the shattering nightmare that upset her most. She was grateful that the details had faded quickly. But she couldn't shake the blind panic, total and uncontrollable as any human instinct. That part she remembered. She was fighting for her life. What could it mean? she wondered. A vision of hell?

Dreams were a rarity in Nancy's life. She could recall none in particular. Even as a child, when hailstones pelted her slate roof like a lunatic drummer and her father would sit by her side, explaining the process in terms of atmospheric inversions and crystallizations, she would finally yawn and fall into a peaceful sleep. He knew when to be so boring, she thought, managing a weak smile at the fond recollection. His lawyer's half-frame glasses balanced at the end of his nose while he solemnly intoned on the science of meteorology. Just his presence was a calming force. God, I miss him, she realized in a flash.

"Bill, I'm sorry. I don't know what happened to me last night. It was all so . . . wrong when it should have been so right."

"I know you've been through a lot. You'll get over it soon enough."

Nancy sensed a touch too much of the philosoper in Addison's voice. You can't expect him to be jumping with joy, she thought, but his tone was irritating nonetheless.

"Dammit, I didn't do it on purpose," she snapped, sick of bottling her feelings. "Of course I wanted to sleep with you. Jesus, I haven't been laid since I got out of that damned hospital. Thank God John isn't interested anymore. Maybe he's into boys all of a sudden. It's just as well, I wouldn't let him touch me either."

"Nancy, I—"

"Please let me finish." Nancy felt like a valve had been opened and she could finally breathe again. "I don't know what the hell is wrong with me. Don't you think I know that last night wasn't the all-American idea of normal for a healthy thirty-year-old woman? First the vestal-virgin routine, then that horrible nightmare. Maybe that was my penalty for letting you down. God, it was awful."

The images burst back like fireworks in her brain. Suddenly she felt like she had just run a ten-mile sprint. Her energy drained away in one long sigh. "But I'm going to find out what's wrong with me. You can believe that."

Bill swerved off the road. He shot out a strong hand just in time to brace Nancy for the jarring stop.

"Now, get this straight," he said in a voice shaking with frustration. "I love you. We're in this together. Your problems are my problems. But you've got to be patient with me. I'm trying to understand. It's a brain-buster. I've never come up against anything like it before. I'm no genius. It's just about all I can do to swallow the fact that you're alive again." His voice trailed off to an intimate whisper. "We'll work it out together. I love you."

Nancy tentatively inched her hand forward until her fingers brushed Addison's knuckles. She fought back her impulse to pull away. Like a swimmer venturing into cold water, she squeezed his hand hard. The sensation of touch brought a feeling of closeness that warmed her body.

"I'm sorry, Bill. I guess you always take things out on the ones you care for most. Who else would put up with so much crap? I don't know what is happening to me. Every time I want you, or think about you, I get a terrible feeling. Like there's a battle going on inside me. The . . . fear is just unbelievable. I can't explain it any other way."

"It'll pass," Addison said with far more conviction than he actually felt. God only knows what happens when you die, he thought. So far He hasn't let us in on that little secret.

"Sure it will," Nancy answered quickly. She knew they were playing a game, but it made her feel better all the same.

"We'll try again, Nancy. Whenever you're ready."

"Soon," she continued the game.

Then it's settled, Addison thought with some relief. He eased the car back on the highway. Trauma, shock, who knows? Maybe it will pass all by itself. Normal sex and no more nightmares, a wonderful life.

A question that had been lingering since the night before popped back into his head. "You called me Willie last night. Since when did you change my name?"

"Willie . . . ?"

"Yes, just as you were waking up."

Nancy blinked with surprise. "I never called you Willie in my life. It's a foolish name for a grown man."

"Well, then, who is Willie?"

"Who's on first?" Nancy shrugged.

Addison turned the key in the lock and paused like a cautious man entering an enemy's territory. He listened, and sniffed the air for hostile vibrations. But the apartment was empty, just as Nancy assured him it would be. Don't be silly, she had told him when he dropped her off. "John's on a week's business trip. He's practically never home anyway. Cryonics, cryonics, cryonics, it's all he thinks about. He's out spreading the gospel according to NAC. Me too, I guess." They had agreed to meet right after she finished taping a television interview. "It's all part of the bargain," she had explained with a good sport's resignation to duty.

Addison felt a rising twinge of jealousy as he began to tour the large apartment. For the first few minutes he managed to tread lightly on the side of propriety that separates a curious guest from a snooper. A peek into the bedrooms, his and hers, to check out the decor. Counting television sets and the other inevitable duplications that mark an unsuccessful marriage. All that was fine. But it wasn't enough. He felt in his gut that there were rocks that needed turning.

It wasn't a conscious thought, more like a nagging itch. Addison could still tell himself aloud that respect for Nancy included her property too. His hands didn't listen. Too many years of poking into other people's business, he mused, while he watched himself with the detachment of an impartial third party. He went around the apartment with the same intensity he would have employed in setting up a security system. Find the weakness. Smell out whatever isn't quite right. Mostly, it's work for the instincts, he told himself. Right-brain stuff. All the electronic gadgetry comes later.

The apartment was clean as an operating room. Every piece of furniture appeared brand-new. He found himself looking for price tags, the way he would in a showroom. There was not so much as a pillow out of place, or a cigarette butt in the ashtrays. The magazines on the coffee table were all the "right" ones and fanned out in a perfect semicircle so all the titles could be read without disturbing the arrangement. It was uncomfortably antiseptic, like a Houston hotel room that had been lowered in place by helicopter and bolted to a concrete slab, one of ten million identical units.

Addison was depressed. He wanted fresh air and the smell of human beings. He was halfway to the door when he decided to leave a note for Nancy. As he expected, a color-coordinated memo pad sat primly beside the telephone. Then a thin smile crossed his face. He had, indeed, found a flaw in the perfect plastic apartment.

The tape on the answering machine was a quarter-inch thick with accumulated messages. Addison tapped his fingers while the rewind hummed. It was a trivial thing, unanswered calls; he knew that well enough. But in the absence of any imperfections at all, it stood out like ice cream on a dung heap.

"Nancy." The voice came out tinny, almost shrill. "Please call me as soon as you come in. My number is . . ." Addison noted it down as he pushed "Fast Forward" for the next message.

"This is Dr. Bundy . . ."

Again.

"This is . . ." Same voice, twice more.

The phone rang. Addison pounced on it.

"Is that you, Dr. Bundy?"

"Yes," came the startled response. "Who is this?"

"Bill Addison. I picked up your messages on Nancy's answering machine. She should be back in a couple of hours. What's wrong?"

There was a long pause. Medical ethics at work, Addison thought. He continued quickly, before Bundy could weigh his loyalties.

"Doctor, I realize we've never met, but Nancy has spoken of you often. Always as a close friend. I feel I can trust you." Let's hope it's mutual, he thought.

"She's told me about you, too, Bill," Bundy responded. A trace of warmth crept into his professional tone. "I look forward to meeting you in person. Now, if you would have Nancy—"

"She changed. I've seen that much for myself." Addison cut him off. His patience with the niceties of medical disclosure were wearing thin. "Do you know something more? Is that why you've been calling?"

"Mr. Addison—"

"Trust me, Dr. Bundy. I love her. I want to help her." Addison held his breath, waiting for a reaction.

"I'm not sure whom to trust." Bundy's voice had the ring of a sad confession. But the curtain drew closed as quickly as it had opened. His professional composure returned. "I'd like Nancy to come in for some additional tests. That's all. Please have her call me."

Addison sensed that his personal appeal was getting no place. "You've already called four times. Isn't that a little heavy for some simple tests? My doctor drops me a slow postcard."

"I'm sure you'll get better service once you've been resurrected," Bundy snapped. "Look here, young man, I've no doubt that your intentions are honorable, but I'm just not prepared to discuss my patient's condition with a layman who isn't even a relative. It wouldn't be proper."

Addison knew he was bumping a stone wall. He would just have to wait for Nancy.

"Tell me this much, Doctor." He let an edge of anger creep into his voice. His question came out like a challenge. "Am I crazy, or has Nancy changed?"

He heard the silence. Then a sigh that could have been surrender. "All right. You're not crazy. Now, will you stop hectoring me and have her call as soon as possible?"

17

Damned unprofessional, Owen Bundy fumed under his breath, talking out of school to a perfect stranger. Yet he had to admit a feeling of relief as he hung up the phone. Addison sees it, I see it, it's bloody plain as day. It's a good thing she's got somebody like him looking over her shoulder. I could certainly use someone looking over mine. He suddenly felt the full weight of his fifty-eight years.

Charts and computer runs covered his wide desk like a pastel smorgasbord. Bloody plain as day to anybody with eyes in his head. The thought brought a pain to Bundy's temples. So why the devil doesn't anything show up on paper? He felt the bubbling frustration of a man attacking a blimp with a hat pin. All those damned tests, and not one concrete thing to show for it.

The random array of papers disturbed his strict sense of medical order and process. He located the folder marked "Seymour" and began shuffling the papers back into place. He saw it as an act of resignation, perhaps defeat. When all else fails, be neat. He was closing the exam book on a course not really learned. Give Dr. Bundy a gentleman's C for Nancy Seymour, and an A+ for neatness. He was disappointed with himself. Blood, urine, EEG, EKG, all the computer lines on thin strips of pink graph paper said that Nancy was fine. Not perfect, Bundy added quickly, far from that. Her weight was down, reaction time had slowed, she had a far lower tolerance for pain. But all that was still within accepted, tolerable limits of decent health. The computers seemed to agree that she was not a sick person.

But computers made their judgments against some unseen, preprogrammed norm. They've never met Nancy Seymour, Bundy mused. She doesn't laugh anymore. There's no joy in her smile. She's frightened and nervous. She's been robbed of her confidence and her drive. It's more then a mood. Addison sees it. Why not those high-priced doctors at NAC? Why not her own husband? The answer that crossed his mind made him glow red with anger. They don't give a damn. They would rather rake in their money than admit that something might have gone wrong. But where? Bundy wrenched his brain. He felt like a lonely swimmer shouting his head off at some distant speck of an ocean liner.

He snapped down his intercom. "Helen, any word from NAC?"

"No, Doctor. I've tried twice. Dr. Stepp is still in conference."

"Try him again, right now."

We must have taken the same tests, he thought. We should have the same information. But NAC has the biggest, most expensive machines. We've finally reached the era of medicine by computer. Still, garbage in . . . garbage out. He listened for the ring, checking his watch. NAC was very late. They should have had their results well before he did. Dr. Stepp had assured him . . .

"Cryonics division," came the crisp salutation.

Damned presumptuous nonsense, he wanted to respond. They have one patient and they start a "division." "Dr. Bundy here," he said instead. "I've been trying to reach Dr. Stepp."

"Yes, Doctor. I'll put you right through."

The unexpected efficiency dulled the edge of Bundy's irritation.

"Owen, how go the wars?" Amos Stepp greeted him heartily. "I was just about to ring you back. Been tied up all morning with business meetings and such. God, I dread those things. I'm a doctor, not an executive. But in today's world it seems that a doctor has to be more than a simple healer," he added philosophically. "Now, what can I do for you, my friend?"

"What can . . . ?" Bundy sputtered. "Nancy Seymour's tests is what. We were going to compare notes. You told me you would have your results by yesterday."

"So I did. Nothing to worry about there. As far as I can tell, she's sound as a dollar. Perhaps a bit overwrought, but that's to be expected."

"I can't fully accept that finding. At least not yet. I was hoping you had come up with something."

"Do you know something I don't?" Stepp asked with a sly intonation.

"It's nothing I can put my finger on. Just a feeling, I suppose. I'm sure all the smart young Harvard Med School doctors at NAC would laugh up their sleeves, but I'm not satisfied with the tests we've taken. The results simply aren't consistent with Nancy's medical history. She isn't sleeping well. Her blood pressure jumped all over the chart. My God, man, all of a sudden she needs glasses. The woman has the night vision of a sixty-year-old. And you tell me there is nothing to worry about. How can you be certain you've cured her military fever? The symptoms are very similar. Doctor, has it occurred to you that you might have removed her from cryonic suspension prematurely?" Bundy grew more excited as he spoke. "I want to know what you've been prescribing for her. Not just now. All along. And I'm going to run some additional tests."

"More tests?" Stepp cut in. "We agreed that the sensible thing was for NAC to run all tests and monitor the results. I've graciously offered you the use of our facilities. There's not a doctor in New York who wouldn't leap at that chance."

"Fine. So long as that does not mean that I am expected to suspend my own professional judgment."

"Do I sense a bit of jealousy, Dr. Bundy? Is that your problem? Want to get your picture in *People* magazine too, do you?"

The remark caught Bundy by surprise. He felt a surge of heat under his collar. "That's absurd. I was her doctor before she ever heard of NAC. She trusts me, and I trust my instincts. There's still more to this business than punching information into a computer. Maybe that's why you can't see the signs that are obvious to me. Now, I would certainly prefer to work with you on Nancy's case, but . . ."

"Dr. Bundy," Stepp said in a voice heavy with disappointment, "may I remind you that Nancy's case is extraordinary. This is not an area for backwoods wisdom. I'm afraid that you are simply not qualified to treat or to evaluate her condition."

"I thought you just got through saying everything was normal, Doctor."

"I did, and it is," Stepp answered curtly. "You'll receive a copy of my analysis, for your files." The line clicked dead, with Owen Bundy still holding the receiver. He was wondering just what it might be that Stepp would not share with him.

Addison shook off his last twinge of guilt. He had given up all pretense of acting the innocent tourist. Now he was ready to start looking in earnest. He started with Nancy's medicine cabinet. The small bottles, stacked atop the larger ones, teetered as he jerked the latch open. He took a step back to count them. Dozens, he guessed. All shapes, sizes, and colors; rinses, tints, creams, and pills. The two bottom shelves were crammed with commercial products packed in flashy cardboard. These he dismissed. It was the smaller bottles with their gray-green typewritten labels that interested him. But even their names were mostly familiar. The dates of the prescriptions went back to 1968. They were the only things in the apartment old enough to gather dust. He carefully replaced the bottles he had examined.

Halfway through the third closet, Addison was ready to give up. They were all the same, the closets, dresser drawers, the entire apartment. Packed and ordered the way an experienced traveler puts together a suitcase for a long trip. No wasted space. No unnecessary items. No dirt or lint. Except for the pill bottles, everything was fresh from the stores. Nancy could have moved in that morning. Doesn't everybody keep some trail back to his past? he wondered.

He heard the lock turn and opened a magazine just in time to toss it aside.

Nancy bolted through the door like a pack of wolves were nipping at her heels. "Never again," she shouted, slamming her purse down on the sofa. "This damned interview was the worst ever. They won't stop picking over me. It's the same questions again and again. Won't they ever believe me when I tell them that I've no memory of being dead? Everybody's looking for the Great Revelation. They're all so disappointed when I can't provide it. Let Stepp cure somebody else. I'm through. Then it took me twenty minutes to find a damned cab. God, I'm sick of this city. Fix me a Scotch, would you, dear? I've got to clean up."

She left the room like a storm that had run its course. Addison poured out two stiff drinks. He was almost certain that it wasn't the interview or the delay that was bothering Nancy. Go easy on Bundy's calls, he decided, but get her to see him.

"Anything else happen at the interview?" he shouted in the general direction she had disappeared.

The answer came back muffled by a closed door. The only words he could make out sounded like "son of a bitch." He decided to drop the subject.

Nancy returned freshly showered and wrapped in a terry-cloth robe. The lines of tension in her face had been washed away with the grime of the streets. Her cheeks were rosy and her smile made Addison smile too.

"Let's go out to dinner," she chimed buoyantly. "I want to stuff myself with pasta."

"That's fine with me. Say, your doctor, Bundy, called while you were out."

"What did he want?" Nancy asked dryly.

"Just that you call him back."

"It'll wait till tomorrow."

"Why don't you call him now." Addison didn't want to sound too pushy. "I couldn't enjoy my dinner knowing that your loyal doctor is hovering by his telephone."

"Worrywart."

But to his relief, Nancy lifted the phone.

"Dr. Bundy, please. This is Nancy Seymour."

She listened for a few moments. "No, it isn't important. I'll call back tomorrow." Then, to Addison, "Hovering by the phone, huh? His answering service says that he's not available. Now can you eat in peace?"

Addison felt his stomach sink like he had just swallowed a heavy stone.

The guard took Willie Garvin's driver's license and jotted down the number in his logbook. Then he dialed the office number Willie had given him. Willie struck his best nonchalant pose, turning his back on the guard as though this sort of visit were an everyday affair. No shuffling, he thought, no shifty glances. In fact, he was checking out escape routes in case the guard's heavy hand came slamming down on his shoulder. It was early enough that the building lobby was still crowded with workers cursing the late commuter trains as they scurried to their elevators. NAC people? he wondered. They rented half the building, so he decided it would be a fifty-fifty chance. Nobody paused to notice him.

The guard tapped him, and Willie jumped.

"You can go upstairs now, buddy. Dr. Victor's expecting you. Thirty-second floor."

He'll forget all about you the minute you've gone, Willie. Just keep believing that, he told himself. Don't let the bastards push you around. Sound advice, he thought, so why the hell are my hands shaking like I've got a bad case of the DT's?

A pert receptionist met him at the elevator. She pointed the way down a long corridor. Gilt-framed oils hung on the walls, but Willie hardly noticed. His feet were walking at a proper pace, but his head was spinning like a dervish. Only the maddening thought of John Victor sitting fat and happy in a plush corner office kept him on course. He wrestled with the part of his brain that was screaming: Get out . . . run . . . you're walking into a lions' cage. They'll eat you alive.

John Victor's secretary had her own office that was larger than Willie's hotel room and furnished with leather and good dark woods. He guessed that the Oriental rug on the floor was worth twice what he earned in a year. The notion firmed his resolve. You'll get your fair share, for Nancy too, he vowed.

The secretary rapped discreetly before opening the door.

"Go right in, Mr. Garvin," she said. Willie detected the hint of a sneer in her voice. Was it his rumpled suit amid the opulence of NAC? he wondered. He worked at being angry. It was better than being frightened.

"Willie, you'd better have a damned good reason for being here," Victor said when he finally got around to looking up from his papers. Willie walked directly to the chair beside his desk. To his amazement and delight he felt his confidence surge. He isn't going to kill me. They're just men after all. Even Stepp. The thought buoyed him.

"You don't scare me, Dr. Victor," Willie blurted out from the confusion of his newly found courage. He instantly regretted his rashness. Victor's dark eyes glared pure loathing.

"We made a bargain, Willie. Why haven't you kept your end?"

"I did," Willie said defensively. "Up to now. But you hurt Nancy."

"What?" Victor exploded. For a moment Willie feared he would leap up from behind his desk.

"I know you did," he added quickly. "I've seen her."

Victor's face turned ashen white.

"Don't worry. She didn't see me. Not yet, anyway." There was just the hint of a threat in Willie's voice.

"She was supposed to be perfect," he continued. "Good as new. No aftereffects. That's what you promised me. Well, she's still just as beautiful. I did my part." A trace of pride crept into his tone and he found himself sitting a bit straighter in his chair. For a moment his fingers could feel the soft texture of Nancy's hair. He breathed in her aroma. Then his hands kneaded her firm thighs like a sculptor smoothing his clay. The memory made him brave.

"Now every time I see her she's going to some doctor. I want to know what went wrong. Nancy is more important than all the money."

"Our part was a little more difficult," Victor responded sarcastically. "Whatever you think you've seen while sneaking around behind her is a figment of your perverted imagination. If you've come here with some idea of shaking me down, you worm, you've got another think coming. Now you've seen me. Get out before I have you arrested."

Willie could see the beads of perspiration forming on Victor's lips and sense the fear that lurked behind the bravado in his voice. He decided to play his trump card.

"I'm not leaving town until I see Dr. Stepp. He's the one who runs the show. Not you. You just work for him. I want him to tell me what's going on. And remember, I know something about cryonics too. You tell him I'll be in touch. I'm not stupid. I know how much money you're making on poor Nancy. He'll see me, or I'll see Nancy."

"You do that, and I'll kill you," Victor said in a hiss of rage. "Now, get the hell out of my office, you blackmailing little son of a bitch."

Fine with me, Willie thought, and managed a smile as he got to his feet. Let Victor be the messenger boy. He'll be sure to cover his own ass first.

Willie was almost at the door when Victor's voice cracked at him like a whip. "Before you do anything very stupid, Willie, remember, you've got problems too. Buried in Brewster."

"Gold." Amos Stepp weighed the word carefully, savoring its sound like a tasty morsel. "Gold is ready for another major move. It's the ideal investment for people going into cryonic sleep. The more rich customers we sign up, the more gold they'll stash away. We could even recommend it." He shook his head thoughtfully. "Maybe that would be a bit much. Anyhow, we shall beat them to the punch and buy it first, cheap."

Victor listened, but his interest was elsewhere. Finance bored him when his mind was calm. Then he would regard it as a bookkeeper's chore. When he was troubled the numbers rose up like trees to block out the sun, and he had no patience at all. It wasn't that he didn't love money. He simply didn't understand the machinations of earning it.

"Turn off that damned ticker tape, Amos. We've got a serious problem," he said when he could stand no more of Stepp's prattle.

Stepp thought it over for a moment before reluctantly flipping the switch on his desktop computer. The keys stopped humming and the CRT froze on its last image: "NAC up 2½. 3 for 1 split anticipated on record earnings."

"Now that you're a rich man, John, you should learn to relax. Take up golf or the stock market. But for God's sake stop fidgeting. It simply isn't becoming."

"Amos, do you know who was up to see me this morning?"

"Willie Garvin?" Stepp asked slyly.

Victor was more irritated than surprised. "Then you also know that he's been sucking around after Nancy. He's a weirdo. God knows what he'll pull. Doesn't that bother you?"

"I expected him to turn up sooner or later. As you correctly if crudely pointed out, Willie is a very disturbed, alienated young man, with very strong feelings for your wife. Did you ever notice the way he looked at her? The worship in his eyes? A homosexual's goddess, I suppose. But I'm confident he'll continue to worship from afar," Stepp answered calmly.

Victor was shocked. "You're going to sit on your ass and do nothing?"

"John, what real harm could Willie cause? His alternatives are limited. He is not without his own blemishes."

"Thank God for small blessings," Victor sighed. "Still, I don't like it one bit. What happens if he does see Nancy and manages to . . . get through to her?"

Stepp began packing folders into his briefcase. "What do you propose, John? Perhaps you'd like to have the little wretch murdered? I mean, it is true that he might interfere with business. Don't you think you're overreacting just a bit?" Stepp asked crisply, making it perfectly clear that he considered the matter closed.

"We haven't settled a damned thing, Amos. Maybe you can shrug Willie off, but I can't."

"I'm not shrugging Willie off," Stepp said with growing impatience. "I have pressing business elsewhere. Willie will just have to wait. Or, better yet, you handle him. Use your best judgment."

"What the hell could be more pressing?" Victor demanded. "You've got to see your damned stockbroker, or Swiss banker or something? I tell you, that little fag could—"

Stepp's eyes turned icy cold and he shot a finger to his lips. Victor knew he was right. The walls had ears.

"If you must know, John, I'm going to take a ride up to Connecticut to see Mr. Kholer. He wants me to explain why we have not been able to repeat our smashing success with your wife. He is, to say the least, displeased. All our tanks are occupied, while ten thousand applicants are panting in the wings. Turnover is what Mr. Kholer wants. Cure 'em, defrost 'em, and freeze the next batch." Stepp was a master at mimicking Arch Kholer's nasal New York accent. "Turnover. More success. Then he'll spring for a few more tanks. Damned shortsighted moron. But, alas, he's my problem."

"What can you tell him?" Victor felt a wave of anxiety. Even a vicarious meeting with corporate authority caused his palms to sweat. He was a man who deep down hated bosses.

"Come along and listen. Maybe you'll forget about Willie Garvin and wake up to Big Business and the bullshit that makes it run. If we get there early, you'll have a few minutes to play in the laboratory."

It was an invitation that John Victor could not turn down. If there was to be a nasty confrontation with Kholer, then he would be a fly on the wall. But he knew Stepp could pull it off. Whatever the problem. Whatever Kholer's mood. Amos Stepp would walk out of that office with the blotter off Kholer's desk if he wanted it. He had done it before. He had taken cryonics from a three-man garage operation somewhere on the back lot, running on a nickel-and-dime NASA grant, to the biggest thing NAC had. When Amos Stepp spoke, Arch Kholer listened, very carefully. Elation shoved aside the clouds of gloomy fear Victor had been carrying like a heavy suitcase. He delighted in watching Stepp in action. But even more, he delighted in playing the master of a multibillion-dollar medical facility.

He could walk through the laboratories at NAC, and second to Amos Stepp, he was the boss. He knew that he had not suddenly grown smarter or begun to work so much harder, he was simply making vastly more money doing the same things. He realized there were many people who could do his job. Make his speeches, talk to the press and concerned senior citizens and anyone else who would listen. But none of them happened to be Nancy Seymour's husband. His road to riches had been bumpy enough to make him appreciate the smooth stretches. Wandering through the laboratory with his thumbs tucked in his vest like a general on inspection was part of the fun.

A sense of anticipation, almost excitement, rose inside him. He watched the miles quietly slip by. Greenwich, Stamford, rolling green Connecticut. Fifteen more minutes to Fairfield. The black-capped driver must have sensed his urgency. He pushed the limousine faster, weaving between the scattered traffic like a worm among pebbles. The laboratory was Victor's real love, and he was almost there. He lit a long cigar and settled back into the limousine's plush rear seat.

"Do you really expect any trouble from Kholer, Amos?" Victor asked amiably.

Stepp looked up sharply as though he, too, had just been

awakened from his private thoughts. "No, no," he mumbled. "I've already taken care of it."

"Then why did you have to rush up here? That doesn't make any—"

"I'm sorry, John," Stepp said quickly. "I thought you said 'Bundy.' "

18

Dispel your anxieties, Victor thought. Face up to things. That's all it takes to send those nameless little fears fleeing to the four winds. He leaned over the guardrail as far as he dared, feeling the splash of vertigo brought on by empty space beneath the soles of one's shoes. It was forty feet down to the gray concrete slab where the tanks were lined up like a small army of life-size tin soldiers. Victor scanned their glistening dome tops. They were a hydra's head for the maze of pipes, tubing, and wires that spouted out. The tubes ran to the liquid nitrogen tanks. Everything else eventually ran into the clicking computer memory banks. Consoles beside each tank displayed the temperature within, as well as a complete medical history, life status of all organs, and disease growth and progress toward a cure. More information constantly flowed from the electrodes attached to the body. Every step of the cryonic process could be traced and analyzed in the greatest possible detail. A medical student's delight, Victor thought. The source of a thousand Ph.D. dissertations. A labyrinth of data to be checked and rechecked, all in the cause of science. He had no doubt at all that the four hundred bodies inside those tanks were subject to far more careful scrutiny dead than they had ever been alive.

He leaned out a bit farther. A few of the technicians who monitored the equipment noticed him and waved. He looked right past them to the clear plastic face masks at the front of each tank. Strain as he would, he was still unable to make out the faces. He knew that being closer would not make much difference. The technicians at ground level could barely see past the churning gray frozen gas that precipitated a permanent fog inside the tank.

Only Nancy's model had come equipped with a totally cosmetic and very expensive exhaust system. Perhaps if we get another celebrity, Victor mused, we could take it out of mothballs. A Walt Disney, or a John Wayne, somebody people would pay to see. Kholer would like that.

Occasionally a technician would blow on the plastic and wipe it off quickly for a better glimpse of the body inside. Then, for a moment, the barest outlines of a face would become visible. Seconds later the fog puffed back to cover a pair of glossy eyes. After a while most of the technicians grew bored with the effort required to look at a dead person. Mostly, Victor knew, they referred to them as "the stiffs," and went about their business. He, for one, had very little curiosity about the condition of an unrestored face after a couple of months of soaking in −280-degree liquid nitrogen. He worried that if he looked closely, he might see Nancy. The vision of her frozen mask, lifelike as a butterfly in amber, still woke him from deep sleep, shaking and soaked with sweat.

He walked quickly, remembering the main reason for his visit to NAC. He knew the way well enough, back to the days the cryonics wing had been a sketch on a designer's table. He had suggested something in a health-spa motif. Stepp liked the idea. Agreed it would create the proper image for cryonics. But Kholer and the budget people had prevailed and the new wing came out looking like a second-rate airplane hangar. What they saved in construction, Stepp managed to wheedle with additional equipment. No shortage there, Victor noted with some satisfaction. More computers to build a better paper maze.

Victor brushed past the security guard. Double doors electronically swung open. He paused to catch his breath. A crowd of white-coated technicians was clustered at the far end of the brightly lit computer room. It occurred to him that someone should have been on duty to check his credentials. Practically anyone could have walked in.

"There you are, John," Stepp's voice boomed out. "Come have a look at this."

He was at the center of the crowd, standing out like a penguin in his dark suit. A crooked finger signaled Victor, but his eyes never left the CRT display. The technicians were gently jostling for position behind him, craning their necks like something important might actually be happening on the small screen. Victor was absolutely certain that they had no idea what they were watching. He had hired most of them.

He slapped a few backs and shook a few hands as the staff shuffled aside to form an aisle.

"What is it, Amos?" he asked.

"Watch this." Stepp punched a code number into the computer console. A closed-circuit-television camera zoomed in on a tank. Its image took up the left half of the CRT screen. The tank became transparent as the computer simulated the body within. Multi-colored points of light corresponding to the nearest organ flashed on the surface of the cadaver like a bad case of prickly heat. The right side of the CRT churned out columns of bright green numbers.

"Mr. Edensword has reached equilibrium," Stepp announced proudly. "Only six hours in the tank and we have destroyed all trace of bacterial growth. That, John, is because we started with the best laser surgery. This body cannot deteriorate any further. Just look at the organ weights. Heart, lungs, kidneys, all within a gram of their recorded weight during body wash."

Victor had observed the body-wash process often enough. It fascinated and amused him. He often thought of the Keystone Kops playing doctor. A freshly dead body was raced into the operating room. Almost instantly a half-dozen masked surgeons, scalpels in hand, descended on it like vultures around a carcass. They made the first small cuts, then the lasers took over for the delicate work. Relatives hated scars when they were forking over big money. Everybody wanted to come out looking like Nancy Seymour, Stepp had observed.

The object of their haste was the fastest possible immersion into cryonic suspension. But first the blood had to be pumped out and all the fluids removed from the vital organs. These were frozen separately, to be reused at the time of reanimation. If the fluids were left in the body, their constituent parts of water would expand upon freezing, bursting thin capillary walls and causing fatal damage to delicate nerve synapses.

The requirement for speed, even in the operating room's totally antiseptic environment, was necessitated by the risk of infection while the body's defense mechanisms were not functioning. You can't be dead, and healthy, Victor noted.

The pumps were then reversed. DMSO was forced through the circulatory system. Antifreeze, Nancy had called it. The name stuck. The DMSO solution had been Stepp's personal triumph. When applied to the skin after the incisions were closed, it not only protected the skin from the worst effects of liquid nitrogen, it healed the incisions to such an extent that practically no scarring was visible. Victor allowed as how that might have been cryonics' strongest selling point. You live again, and you are still pretty.

Stepp turned to the assembled technicians. "Good work, gentlemen."

These guys just push buttons and watch gauges, Victor thought with disgust. They'd puke if they ever had to get next to a real gamy dead body.

"Keep it up," Stepp continued jovially. "And we'll all have a hell of a nice profit-sharing package come year end. And don't think Mr. Kholer doesn't know the kind of job you people are doing. John . . ." He got up and gestured toward the door.

Victor waited until they were halfway down the long corridor before he spoke. Even then he looked around twice. "Why do you patronize them, Amos?" he whispered. "They don't even know what's going on."

"It's good for morale, John. You'll never be a first-class executive until you understand morale. A general reviews his troops. A division head meets his employees. It's all the same. Pump them up. Get the teamwork bubbling. Make them proud of cryonics and NAC. My visits have an incalculable effect on morale."

"Who gives a shit?"

"My, you're in a waspish mood, John. Not good stuff when you're going to see the Big Enchilada. Get your mind off Nancy. Think of money. Be cheerful. Be positive."

You pompous jerk, Victor boiled to respond, but the elevator had come. Elevators at NAC were wired with highly sensitive microphones as well as the standard complement of television cameras. Nobody talked in the elevators.

It was a short ride. Four floors up, then down another long corridor. Like most suburban office complexes, the sprawl was lateral rather then vertical. This corridor was expensively carpeted, setting off the dark-wood-paneled walls and occasional potted palms. No tile floors and bare-faced red brick for the Big Enchilada, Victor thought. He watched Stepp's confident gait and tried to emulate it. But somehow the money didn't seem real, and he could barely fake cheerful, let alone positive. His feet were itching and he had a yen to run. The touch of Stepp's hand on his shoulder shocked him like an ice cube down the back. Stepp's grip tightened as he steered him toward the men's room.

"Amos, what are you—?" Victor protested.

Stepp put a finger to his lips while he discreetly peeked into each stall. Only when he was satisfied they were alone did he nod back to Victor. "Run the water," he instructed.

"Amos, I'm all right. Really."

"No you're not, John. I know you. There lurks deep in your weasel-hearted nature an unfortunate chord of all-American decency. I must admit that I suspected this when I hired you. But I, too, have flaws. Mine, being arrogance, made me assume that science and a decent sense of your best interests would give you sufficient reason to keep your wits. Now I'm beginning to have my doubts." Stepp's shoulders seemed to grow heavier as he paced before the gushing sinks. Finally he stopped directly in front of Victor and tilted his head back to look the taller man in the eye. "John, do you still love your wife? Be frank. God knows it's perfectly natural. She's a lovely girl. But you can't be a sentimentalist. The days of whirlwind courtship are long since past. You knew you'd have to put all of that behind you. Your personal life is no longer important. Your work comes first. Never forget it. One slip and everything is gone."

Victor's surge of anger made his heart pound and turned his cheeks a glowing red. He knew there was nothing he could say. Stepp's warning had given him a vision of his hard-won profits slipping into a fog of frozen nitrogen.

"Amos, maybe I'm just pissed off," Victor admitted. "Here I am making all this money and I still have to sit back with my mouth shut while that son of a bitch Addison screws my wife. It's so demeaning. When this is all over, I'm going to pound his face into mush."

The remark brought a thin smile to Stepp's coarse features. It was just the reaction Victor had expected. They both knew he had absolutely no intention of going anywhere near Bill Addison.

"All right, John, I'll buy that. When the project is completed, you can do as you like," Stepp responded. "But you're going to have to pull up your socks before we go in to see Kholer. The old man is really breathing fire."

Not far off the mark, Victor thought anxiously as he crossed and uncrossed his legs, seeking the elusive comfortable position. Kholer's chairs were the sleek modern Italian version of a barber chair. They slanted so steeply that his knees were level with his chest and his ass sank in the middle like an anchor. He was convinced that the chairman knew just how uncomfortable they were when he ordered them. Stepp avoided the problem by pacing the length of the office. Kholer drummed his fingers on his desk, waiting for the return leg of his march.

". . . Your concerns are legitimate, Arch." Stepp's sonorous tones tinkled the crystal chandelier. "But we've always been scrupulous in our advertising: *when* and *if* we cure the disease—only then can we revive the patient. We never gave anybody a delivery date. We're talking about science. Science can take its stubborn time about handing over a guarded secret."

"The hell we're talking about science, Amos. Don't muddy the water with me." Arch Kholer glared out from under his bushy eyebrows. He had learned how to debate in the style of a wrestler charging his opponent. He saw that he had a clear shot at the cryonics division. Profits aside, it galled him that any area of his corporation could operate without his direct supervision. Yet, little as he personally liked the man, he allowed that Amos Stepp was far too valuable an asset to lose. Perhaps director of corporate planning, he mused, once this cryonics furor blows over a bit. "We're talking about business, Amos. I've got your proposal to finance a hundred more of your fabulous tanks and I'm telling you that this time it just won't fly. You're not getting another dime out of NAC until you move out some of those stiffs you've got pick-

ling in there now. The board needs some fresh results. The
market needs it too. Nancy Seymour is old news. You don't
even see her on the Donahue show anymore." He turned and
nodded perfunctorily at Victor. "No offense, JV. Just straight
talk."

"That's what we're here for, Arch." Victor thought the
phrase sounded very executive.

Kholer ignored it, returning his full attention to Stepp.
"Crapola aside, Amos, when the hell are you going to defrost
somebody else? I'm starting to get some heat from the board.
They want you to publish that final paper on the process and
get the SEC out of our hair. Personally, I'd stall for years on
the damned thing. Let the bastards sue us. Why the hell
should Merck and Abbott labs be able to use our research? It
would be so damned much easier, Amos, if you'd just bring
somebody else back from the dead," he said like a man
asking for a five-dollar loan.

Victor was not surprised. He understood enough about
business to know this day had to come. It was all a matter of
turnover. They were holding deposits for a waiting list that
could stretch into the twenty-first century. The public wants
action or a new toy, he thought.

"Our research people are looking into some very interesting things, Arch," Stepp said confidently. He had dealt
with churlish directors before.

Kholer looked him square in the eye. "That's fine, Amos.
As long as you are so close to getting results, I'm sure you'll
understand why I've felt compelled to buy television time
. . . to bring the public up-to-date. Now I can add that our
research department is confident that we will be able to accel-
erate the program shortly."

Stepp gasped. "You can't be serious, Arch. I won't be responsible for any such statement."

"Amos, NAC is a business, not a government grant or
damned charity," Kholer shot back. "Cryonics has to pay its
way. You can't live off one success forever."

"Fair enough." Victor was amazed by the forceful ring of
his own voice. "Cryonics is the science of the future, Arch. If
it takes a bit longer for that future to get here, well, so be it.
In the meanwhile, you've got your stockholders to look after."

"Well put, JV." Kholer shook his head approvingly.

Stepp was clearly puzzled, and very angry. At first Victor enjoyed watching him stew. They had not spoken for the rest of the meeting, or halfway back to New York. Stepp grumbled to himself as he savaged the papers from his briefcase, scribbling huge red notes on the tops of the neatly typed memos balanced on his lap. Victor was growing tired of his act. He was prepared to tolerate Stepp's bad manners in public. That was part of their bargain. Stepp was the boss. But the same antics in private offended Victor's sense of honesty. He tapped the intercom between themselves and the front seat to make sure the chauffeur could not hear them.

"Amos, by my reckoning we've netted about twenty million dollars to date. That doesn't even count what we've made personally on the stock and options. How much more did you think we could squeeze out?"

"Don't make things any worse between us, John. You could have said something helpful back there, or nothing at all. But, no, you had to take Kholer's side. If only he'd given us those tanks and a little more time."

Victor was shocked. For a moment he did not believe Stepp was serious. He was about to speak, but the grim set to Stepp's jaw made him hold his peace. They had already succeeded beyond his wildest expectations. Anything more struck him as piggishly irrational and dangerous. "Have it your own way, Amos."

"You don't understand, John. We must carry on," Stepp said quietly. His anger had vanished.

Victor's instincts warned him not to argue. "Just what I was thinking, Amos. No time to quit now."

"Don't patronize me, you fool. And you can stop scheming about sneaking off to Brazil with all your newfound money. I've been forced to take measures that would make a sudden departure most embarrassing. Don't you see, John, we've almost got it licked. Cryonics can work."

19

The long brightly lit room with its hundreds of small win-
dowed cages reminded Addison of an old nickel-slot Auto-
mat. He followed closely behind the balding thin man whose
pace hardly gave him time for a glance around. Everything
was sparkling clean, and except for their footfall on the tile
floor, absolutely quiet. There was not an odor or speck of
dust in the air. Occasionally his guide would pause and make
a brief comment. Addison wanted to concentrate, but his
thoughts kept slipping back to Nancy. It had been a last-
minute decision. He almost hadn't come to Washington. Yet
he knew this was an opportunity he could not pass up. It had
taken a week of string-pulling just to get a security clearance
that would allow him past the front door at the Johns
Hopkins cryonic-research laboratory. They too, he found out,
were part of the NASA manned space program.

"Now, here's a nifty little show-stopper, Bill." The thin
man abruptly halted and jabbed a bony finger at the nearest
cage. A brown guinea pig lay curled in a frozen fetal position. Addison saw nothing to distinguish this one from the
hundreds they had already passed. He waited for Dr. Tim
Bendel to make his point. The assistant research director

rapped his knuckles on the cage. "You see, Bill," he continued, "we've actually brought this one back from the dead."

"I don't think you've brought him back far enough, Tim."

Bendel broke into a wide smile. "I see what you mean. Sam's under again for a new round of tests. If we bring him back a second time he'll be the world's champ. A dumb guinea pig will break Nancy Seymour's record. The public will love that one. Then maybe we'll be able to get a couple of bucks from Uncle."

Addison sensed the real annoyance in Bendel's light remarks. It had been a long while since anyone but NAC had gotten more than table scraps for cryonic research.

"I'll bet you're still doing better than you ever expected. NAC brought the high rollers into the game. Who the hell ever heard of cryonics until Nancy Seymour started plugging it on TV? Now everybody with an ice pick wants to go public and get a government grant," Addison prodded. He felt Bendel had a lot more to tell him.

They had reached the end of the specimen-storage facility. Bendel shoved open the double doors that led to a deserted elevator corridor. Addison feared he was growing weary of playing the tour guide.

"Bill, my instructions to cooperate come right from the director. I suspect you have some very well-placed friends. I want to do what I can to help you. It's just that I'm not sure I know what you're after. You've seen our labs. You've seen our puny version of the famous tank. You met Sam." Bendel turned to look Addison square in the eye. "That, my friend, is the whole show. So where do we go now?" he asked with the tone of a man who truly wanted to help.

How does it work? Addison almost blurted out. How does it change you? Hopkins was the third cryonic facility he had seen in the past six weeks. His frustration rose with each visit. They were all so similar in approach. They all used tanks. They all used the same jargon of "body washes" and "organ maintenance" that could have come from an Amos Stepp press release. And they all experimented with animals. All except NAC. The other cryonic facilities measured success in terms of organs reanimated. NAC could bring human beings back from the dead.

"Was NAC just lucky, Tim? Is that what I'm supposed to believe? Stepp pushed all the right buttons and for once the damned thing worked?" To Addison, a system functioned or it did not. Science was constant and predictable. "How come NAC can bring back people while you guys are sweating over a rat? And all with basically the same gear."

"A person, Bill. Not people," Bendel retorted. "They've got a lot of people in storage, but only one has come back. Look, sometimes Uri Geller bends the nail, sometimes he doesn't. We don't have all the answers. I'm a microbiologist. I know the cryonic theory works on paper. So does Amos Stepp. I've read every damned thing he's published. It's a mountain full of little caves. I'm supposed to be an expert, and I don't understand it all. No reason why I should. Stepp has been doing cryonic research for twenty-five years. The work he did for NASA in the sixties was so far ahead of its time that half the scientific community had him pegged as a loony. And the other half ignored him. I think he hated that most of all. He was talking in terms of suspended animation for fifty-year space missions. That was science fiction to the rest of us. He was the first one to develop a DMSO solution for body washouts. Before that everybody was stumped because blood contained too much water. You just can't freeze it inside the body. But you have to use something to keep the arteries from caving in. Stepp found the right mixture. Bill, cryonics is his life's work. He was bringing back whole organs, intact, while we were still playing with cells. I grant that maybe now that he's making a bundle of money he's holding back on some key part of his process. Letting the rest of us sweat it out for a while. Just like he had to. I can't say I blame him. The mere fact that we have not been able to duplicate his results does not, in my judgment, refute his claims. Certainly not yet."

"What could go wrong, Tim? Could there be side effects or some permanent changes?" Addison had listened to the scientist's noble side. Now he wanted a bit of Bendel's jealousy to seep out.

Bendel peered carefully over the tops of his half-frame glasses. Then he drew Addison close, as though there were a crowd that might be listening. "The director told me that you wanted background on cryonics for personal reasons. You're not a journalist, are you?"

"I'm a friend of Nancy Seymour."

Bendel turned bright red. "Say, I'm sorry if I said anything out of line. I just—"

"Forget it." Addison knew he had timed it right.

"Okay, just so long as my name never comes up."

Addison nodded his agreement.

"Bill, as far as I'm concerned, nobody in this field knows exactly what the hell they're doing. You want to know about side effects while we're all groping in the dark. Even Dr. Stepp. In total, the vast science of cryonics has got Nancy Seymour, one guinea pig, and a refrigerator full of kidneys and spleens that we've brought back from the deep-freeze. It's potluck. We don't even know an organ's specific tolerance for cold. Neither does Stepp, only he won't admit it. If I went off like this in public it would sound like sour grapes."

"I'm not the public, Tim. I still don't see why NAC can, and the rest of you guys can't," Addison said bluntly.

"A successful cryonic process is more than a simple matter of keeping the meat fresh. Chipping a twenty-thousand-year-old mastodon out of a block of artic ice and hacking off a couple of dozen fresh steaks is a neat trick, but it does not scientifically account for Nancy Seymour's live act. Organ tissue must deteriorate in the presence of severe cold. NAC froze Nancy in liquid nitrogen. That's about three hundred degrees below zero. It has to be that cold. Any warmer and you invite bacterial growth. Everybody agrees that would be fatal. But steel turns to powder at that temperature. DMSO or not, I can't believe that nothing happens to plain flesh at that temperature."

"I've read some of Stepp's papers too, Tim. He claims the DMSO works. It buffers the skin."

"Very good. You've done some homework. We've had some success with DMSO too. Just not to the same degree." Bendel's voice trailed off. He beat his fist into his palm for a moment. Something had stuck in his mind. "I'd like you to come to my office. Perhaps it is all just a matter of degree."

Dr. Bundy's voice had been bland as a stock quote. Nancy played the tape back in her mind, hoping for some inflection that would give a clue to his purpose. Her sharpest intuition could infer nothing. After a night of stewing, she could barely wait to see him. It's got to be good news, Bill had reassured her. Bundy's found something. You'll be back to your old self in no time. You'll be happy again. Nancy allowed for the possibility. That was as far as she would speculate. She only wished Bill could have stayed a bit longer. She felt a surge of affection every time she thought of him. The doorman turned around as she stepped out into the crisp morning air.

"Taxi, Miss Seymour?"

Nancy nodded, staring up the traffic-clogged avenue. A good pair of sneakers would have served her better than a car. The doorman let loose an ear-shattering blast from his whistle. He had positioned himself in the middle of the street, hunched slightly forward like a football player poised to tackle the first available vehicle. A moment later a taxi swerved to a halt in front of her awning. The pace and noise distracted Nancy from her own thoughts.

"Twenty-one Gramercy Park South," she called through the driver's open window. Suddenly speed seemed vital to her. She wanted to be downtown before the start of Dr. Bundy's patient hours. The driver saw an opening in the traffic and took off like a quarter-mile dragster. Nancy found that just the act of moving quickly was sufficient to buoy her spirits.

A smile crossed her lips. Perhaps there's a pill, she mused. Dr. Bundy's found the pill and there will be no more bad dreams, no more fears. She was still smiling when she walked into Dr. Bundy's waiting room.

Something was wrong. The straight chairs that lined both walls were empty. A rosy-cheeked nurse looked mildly surprised as she glanced up from her file cards.

"Miss Seymour . . . you don't have an appointment, do you?"

Nancy moved close enough to read her nameplate. She was embarrassed to have forgotten the name that went with the familiar face. "No, Mrs. Glick, but Dr. Bundy phoned me last night. He told me to come in." Nancy could hear the urgency bubbling up in her voice.

"You spoke to Dr. Bundy last night?" Nurse Glick asked with marked surprise.

"I didn't actually speak with him, Nurse. He left a message on my answering machine. He said he had some important information for me. May I see him?"

"I'm sorry, Miss Seymour. The doctor won't be in today,"

the nurse said softly. She wanted to ease the shock she saw rising in Nancy's eyes.

"What? Where is he? I must speak with him."

"Miss Seymour," she said firmly, while she laid a gentle hand on Nancy's arm, "I'm afraid that won't be possible. If you require immediate medical attention I can refer you to Dr.—"

"No." Nancy felt a cold chill up her back. She realized she was shouting. "It's Dr. Bundy I want. Where is he? You must tell me."

"Honestly, Miss Seymour, I've no idea myself. His service notified me yesterday that he would be unavailable. There was no further message. I cancelled all his appointments, but your name wasn't on the list."

The nurse skillfully led Nancy to a sofa beside Bundy's door.

"You just sit here until you feel better, Miss Seymour. Is there anything I can get you, a cup of tea perhaps?"

Nancy shook her head numbly. She felt as though the bottom had fallen out of her stomach.

"When will he be back?" she mumbled.

"Are you sure you're all right, Miss Seymour? You don't look at all well." The nurse held Nancy's limp wrist lightly between her fingers. Then she cradled Nancy's chin, tilting her head upright to check the dilation of her pupils.

"I think I'd best call your husband, Dr. Victor," she said with a ring of concern.

"No," Nancy said as adamantly as she could. "He's out of town," she stammered on.

The nurse's brow wrinkled. She studied Nancy with a worried, skeptical eye. Nancy forced herself to sit erect and managed a weak smile to mask her fear and frustration. Undependability was so unlike Dr. Bundy. She simply could not picture the man who had been a friend all her adult life casually taking a day off, knowing her sanity might be hanging by a fragile thread. The nurse's explanation rang hollow. Is this some kind of horrible test? she almost blurted out. Instead she managed a tactful silence.

"If you insist . . ." the nurse relented at last. "But you still don't look well to me. Your skin is clammy, and your pulse rate is way up. Go into the doctor's office and lie down for a few minutes."

How could Owen do this to me? Nancy wondered frantically. Just not show up. . . . She used her anger like a crutch, to straighten her knees and help herself up. Mrs. Glick took her hand, leading her gently, like a child, from the brightly lit waiting room, through the dark wood door, into Bundy's somber, very familiar office. It was just as Nancy had seen it last. She made her own way to the leather sofa. "I'll be all right now," she managed evenly.

"Would you like a cup of tea, Miss Seymour? It's no trouble. I was about to make some for myself."

"No. Thank you."

"Lie quietly until you're feeling stronger. I'll look in on you in a few minutes. If you need anything, just shout. I'll be right outside."

Nancy lay back, staring up at the ceiling through the dust-flecked light from the large window behind Bundy's desk. There's nothing more you can do, she told herself. Be calm. Owen will return. She realized she was breathing the faint odor of Bundy's pipe tobacco that lingered in the furniture and clung to the heavy drapes. Her anger drained away. Only disappointment remained. Mrs. Glick's typing had ceased. The click of her heels told Nancy she was off to the supply room. Tea was ready.

Nancy listened closely. The office was silent.

She slipped behind Bundy's desk, feeling just a little sneaky as she settled into his well-worn swivel chair. But there was a tingle of excitement too. A righteous curiosity overwhelmed her vague ethical qualms. She told herself it was the sort of thing reporters did all the time. She scanned the desktop. The usual jumble of papers had been neatly tucked into a small stack of manila folders. Mrs. Glick's work, Nancy assumed. She automatically checked the half-dozen tabs. Her name was not among them. Dr. Bundy kept his current files in the large bottom drawer. Nancy had watched him often enough to be certain of that much. It's not like stealing, she reasoned as her fingers closed on the brass knob. She had already made up her mind.

The drawer slid open with barely a squeak, but to Nancy's nervous ear it sounded like an express train skidding over wet rails. Her eyes shot up. She held her breath. The only thing she heard was her heart pounding. The dim light forced her to squint. She leaned forward to read the names on the files.

Seymour. It had the girth of a phone book. Nancy turned her chair to the window. The file sat heavily on her lap. Suddenly her hands began leafing through the pages as though they had a will of their own. She skimmed over the sections marked "clinical history," "diagnosis," "visits," "notes." More notes. She was amazed by the detail of Bundy's entries. The latest was October 2, two weeks past. She vividly recalled her last visit. But why the urgent phone calls? She was certain there would be some note. Bundy writes down everything, she thought. Everything. She fanned through the rest of her file. Then she vigorously shook the binder for any loose scraps of paper. Nothing fell out.

Her eyes shot up. Nurse Glick stood jaw agape in the doorway.

"Miss Seymour, what ever are you doing? Those files are Doctor's property. They're confidential."

"He writes down everything," Nancy shouted back. She slammed the file down on the desk with both hands. It cracked like a gunshot. The nurse jumped back. Nancy could see the fear in her eyes.

"Where is Dr. Bundy?" she demanded, storming toward the nurse. "I want the truth."

The nurse spun around and bolted from the office, slamming the door shut behind her. Nancy heard a key turn in the lock. She froze, listening hard to the nurse's muffled tones.

She's phoning John, Nancy realized. He'll bring Stepp along like a hound dog panting on his leash. Nancy was surprised by the depth of her reaction. Still, she could not doubt her feelings. The mere thought of Dr. Stepp made her skin turn cold. She could not bear the thought of being used again. Stepp made her feel helpless, like another balance-sheet asset for NAC. Whatever she sensed her debt might be, she knew that any real gratitude had long since dried up.

Her eyes darted around the office as though it were a cage. It was the first time she noticed the bars on the windows.

The door to Bundy's examining room stood slightly ajar. Nancy made for it. Old buildings provided rear exits. She brushed past the examining table and stopped cold. The back door stood right in front of her just at the end of a short hallway. She ignored it. Something else gripped her attention.

"Nurse Glick," she called out, dismissing the incident that had caused the nurse to flee for her safety. "Come quickly."

The bright overhead lights confirmed her first reaction. The paper on the examining table was ripped and crumpled shabbily. The glass front of the medicine cabinet was smudged with palm prints like a child's cookie jar. She knew the examining room like part of her own home. The sloppiness stood out like a misplaced sofa in the living room. Dr. Bundy was rigorously tidy in his clinical procedures.

Nancy pulled her address book out of her purse. She had Bundy's unlisted home number. She looked up with a start. The heavy lock on the office door had turned open.

"Miss Seymour," the nurse called cautiously. "Are you all right? You gave me quite a fright, you know."

A man had entered just behind her. Nancy felt a wave of relief the moment she realized it was not her husband or Amos Stepp.

"Who else has been in here, Nurse?" Nancy demanded sharply.

"Only you, Miss Seymour."

"No. Dr. Bundy would never leave an examining room in that state. Who is the last patient he saw? Why isn't my file up-to-date?"

Nancy noticed that the man had separated himself from the nurse. He was moving quietly toward her. He was small, with a dark, heavy mustache, and he nodded his head as she spoke. Nancy shot a finger at him. He froze as though caught in a spotlight.

"Who are you?" she asked suspiciously.

"This is Dr. Arthur Latimer," Nurse Glick answered. "I called your husband and he took care of everything. Dr. Latimer was right around the corner, at Bellevue."

"Don't be upset," Dr. Latimer said softly. "I've known John for years. I feel like I know you myself. Now, why don't we just lie down for a few minutes?"

"You're a shrink? My husband sent a shrink. What a jerk."

"I'm sure he knows best, Nancy." Latimer continued to nod his head. "He tells me that you've been having quite a number of these violent outbursts. He's very concerned."

"Concerned about his stock options, maybe." Nancy walked past Latimer, on her way toward the door. "What concerns me right now is the whereabouts of my own doctor.

If neither of you is interested in helping me, I'll find him my-self."

The nurse caught Nancy's arm. Latimer jumped in front to block her path. "I'm afraid you're in no condition to be out on your own, Nancy," Latimer said.

Nurse Glick's grip was as strong as a man's. With one deft twist she had Nancy's jacket off her shoulder.

"I truly hoped this wouldn't be necessary, Nancy," Latimer intoned solemnly, cradling a small syringe lightly in his right hand.

"What are you doing?" Nancy shouted. Suddenly she real-ized she was a prisoner.

"John alerted me that you might be . . . difficult. You can't control your behavior, Nancy. If we're to help you, we must look after your physical safety first."

Nancy barely listened to the words. It was the soothing cant of Latimer's patter that made her cease struggling against the nurse's grip. Then she saw the needle gleam in the dusty light. Latimer squeezed the plunger of the syringe until a drop of fluid glistened at the tip.

"Dr. Latimer, you can't . . ." she pleaded.

"Of course I can," he responded calmly. "For your own good."

Nancy felt the needle's sting in her arm. She tried to clench her teeth but her jaw was suddenly too heavy to budge. The room grew dark and silent like a nightmare re-lived. She feared the people around her. Drugged and stunned, she summoned her last bit of strength. For a mo-ment the office returned to focus and the static in her ears faded back.

". . . a terrible shame." She heard Nurse Glick while vaguely sensing her body being moved like piece of furniture.

"Poor John," Latimer answered. "Only a couple of weeks ago we were all so sure she was cured. It's more than a per-son should have to suffer."

Nancy's brain reeled with confusion. Was she suffering, she wondered, or was it John? The darkness closed in around her.

Victor tugged Stepp's sleeve to hurry him along. Stepp was busy examining the dingy corridor like a general on in-spection tour. With hands clasped behind his back and his nose upturned to catch the mixed aromas of antiseptic and urine, he appeared content to pass an evening amid the grime that surrounded them. Orderlies pushing stretchers double-timed from both directions. Noise and static crackled out of cardboard squawk boxes and bounced off the dirty tile walls that Victor likened to a subway men's room, not a hospital. He was embarrassed.

"For Christ's sake, Amos, this isn't a sightseeing tour. My wife is in this place."

"Don't fret, John." Stepp seized on Victor's mood. "We're the only ones who know she's here. Your friend Latimer had the discreet good sense to admit her as a Jane Doe. The man has management potential."

"Well, how the hell long do you think we can keep it quiet, Amos?" Victor whispered, dodging a phalanx of milling patients in seedy hospital-issue bathrobes.

"Long enough," Stepp replied confidently.

The corridor branched left and right. Victor was sure he could see the horizon drop. His frustration grew as he puzzled over a directory of wards. To his relief, Latimer popped out of a doorway directly in front of him.

"Arthur!" Victor shouted over the din of activity.

"Nancy is all right," was Latimer's immediate response. He mistook Victor's nervousness for concern. "But I'm glad you're here, John."

"Is she in there?" Victor asked anxiously.

"Yes. She's still under sedation. I'm glad you alerted me to her condition. The nurse told me she had been acting very erratic, even violent."

Victor shook his head sympathetically. "We've gone through it before, Arthur. These outbursts were an intermediate phase of her military fever. Then her coordination began to break down. God, that was even more pathetic. I never thought it would happen again."

Stepp pried himself between the two men and thrust an open hand at Latimer. "Dr. Amos Stepp, Dr. Latimer. I think you've handled this unfortunate incident very gracefully. By the way, just what was it that set Nancy off?"

The question was innocent enough to Latimer's ear. Unlike Victor, he was unaccustomed to seeking motives in Stepp's ingratiating guile.

He wants Latimer to repeat what I've already told him, Victor surmised. He knew better than to interfere.

"Nothing at all, really," Latimer answered. "Her GP didn't show up for an appointment."

"Why not?" Stepp asked.

Latimer shrugged. "I didn't bother to ask his nurse. It didn't seem important at the time."

"No, of course not." Stepp thoughtfully stroked his chin. At this point, the best thing would be to release Nancy to her husband. If we are dealing with a relapse of military fever, then she ought to be back at NAC. We have far superior tropical-medicine facilities. Besides, I'm sure we all agree that Bellevue is no place for Nancy to wake up."

"My feelings exactly," Latimer responded. "Just wait here. I'll have Admitting prepare the forms. John, you'll have to sign her out."

"Would you hurry them along, Arthur?" Victor's voice quivered. "We've taken the liberty of ordering an ambulance from NAC. It'll be waiting at the Twenty-seventh Street side."

Latimer took off smartly down the corridor. Stepp watched him out of sight before quietly pushing open the door to Nancy's room.

The light bulb dangled above Nancy's head. Its brightness burned her eyes. That pain, more than anything she could actually see, immediately alerted her. It was the same pain each time the nightmare began. Fear crept through her. She knew without trying to move a muscle that her body would be frozen. She knew the dark man would be coming soon. But this time half her brain was aware of the dream. She could fight it. She could force herself awake like a diver struggling for the surface.

Her willpower was winning. She lifted herself out of her body. For the first time she could see her entire room. It was sparse as a monk's cell, lit only by the hot bare bulb. But from above, the light was softer. She studied her own body lying directly beneath her. The sight made her sob with pity. Her face was a bloodless white death mask with lips withered into thin ridges. She searched for some sign of life behind her puffy closed eyes, but not so much as a lash flickered. The sheet that covered her frailness was more shroud than blanket.

Muffled footsteps padded down the hallway. Her door was ajar. It was happening again, exactly as before. Only this time she could see it all. The footsteps grew sharper. One more step and she knew the floorboard would creak. It did. She squeezed her eyes shut, but the dream would not release her. Not to see was even more frightening. She looked again. A huge man stood stock-still beside her slab. His dark shadow fell across her body. Then his hands began to slowly peel away her sheet. She watched her eyes begin to flutter open. A bolt of fear traveled up from the bed like electricity. Suddenly she saw the dark shape from two angles at once. From the bed he was a shadow, silhouetted against the bright light. But she could see the back of his head and his brawny shoulders as he leaned forward. His breath was hot and he smelled of . . . She knew the smell. It was at the tip of her tongue. His hands went to his belt. He undid his trousers. They dropped to the floor and he stepped out of them, naked from the waist.

Nancy gasped. She felt a cold chill as he slowly peeled back her sheet. Thick fingers kneaded her flesh. Then his hands found their way beneath her back and legs and he scooped her up like a rag doll. His mouth covered her with wet kisses. His hot breath was sucking the air from her lungs. She was suffocating. She screamed. The noise reverberated at a glass-shattering pitch through the small room.

Two nurses burst past Victor, who stood frozen in the doorway. Nancy sat up ramrod-stiff. Her glassy eyes were staring right at Victor all the while she was screaming. He had heard the identical scream once before. He hoped to God that she could not recognize him through the nightmare's grip that still held her fast. Faint, Nancy, he pleaded inside. Just this time. Remember nothing.

The nurses slapped her wrists frantically. Her skin was clammy white. Perspiration and tears streamed down her cheeks. Victor edged closer to listen for the sounds of her labored breathing. It came in short, painful gasps. He knew she was slipping into shock.

"Scopolamine," he said in a hoarse whisper.

The nurse looked at him in total disbelief.

Stepp clamped his hand down hard on Victor's shoulder. "Put her on oxygen immediately," he ordered. The nurse already had the mask in place. Nancy began to breathe more easily. "What the devil has Latimer been giving her?" Stepp asked, hoping the nurse would take Victor's slip as a premature answer. "Did you bring Miss Seymour's release papers?" he continued.

Nancy's eyes widened. For just a moment the blurred figures came into sharp relief. She knew, without hearing the words, that they had come for her. Her husband was devoted. He wanted to help her. She watched Dr. Stepp writing something at the bottom of a form. Why didn't she want to be helped? She began to shake her head from side to side, faster and faster. The nurse took her hand. It did not matter. She knew they would do nothing.

"It's all attended to, Doctor," the second nurse said curtly.

Stepp moved close to Nancy and smiled reassuringly. Her hand shot out defensively in front of her body.

"Nancy, dear, we know what is best," he said in a very reasoned tone. "We're taking you back to NAC. You'll be much more comfortable."

She knew where they were taking her. NAC. That old dingy place where cold drafts rattled the windows. In her mind's eye she saw the gleaming white chrome-and-glass edifice set atop a rolling hill. Both views were real. She had to speak. She unstrapped her oxygen mask. Stepp's hand brushed her ear and touched her at the nape of her neck. He squeezed hard for just a moment. Her shout was trapped before it could reach her lips. She slumped forward, unconscious.

"A bit of pressure on the occipital nerve. Much quicker then Pentothal. Safer, too, in the long run," Stepp said casually.

"You didn't have to do that, Amos." Victor was stunned. He knew things like that happened in state mental institutions, but he had never actually seen it. That his wife was the victim upset him to the same degree as any similar undignified spectacle. He simply did not like a mess. "She was ready to come along," he added. He would have said more, but nobody was listening. Two orderlies from NAC had rolled their stretcher beside the bed. Under Stepp's watchful eye they quickly and gently slid Nancy over. It was just as well they had come when they did. Stepp's hard glare warned him that he had already said enough. As he backed out into the corridor he observed that one of the nurses had remained to hold Nancy's hand while the orderlies rolled her out. He had never felt like such a coward or quite so miserable in his entire life.

He watched Nancy's eyes as she passed, searching for a sign of love or trust. She did not even blink. For a moment he saw the television image of a younger Nancy, filled with energy and drive. She could do anything. She had a future then, Victor mused. But so did I. It wasn't supposed to work out quite this way.

They followed some distance behind the ambulance. The last stragglers of the evening rush hour kept their speed well below the limit. But for Stepp's nervous foot tapping, Victor would have welcomed the delay. He sensed nothing but trouble waiting for him at the end of the trip.

"We can't just pack Nancy off to NAC forever," he said finally, breaking a half-hour of silence. "She's a celebrity. As soon as her little Bellevue visit leaks out, the press will be all over us."

"The press, Kholer nagging for results, and four hundred patients incurably frozen stiff. Problems, problems," Stepp replied with a good humor that yanked Victor out of his doldrums. "It's almost time to fold our tent, John."

"What are you talking about?"

"John, as they say in the garment district, vee could use a nice little fire."

20

"You're sure there were no calls for me?" Bill Addison asked.

The desk clerk politely set aside his file cards and turned to inspect the block of cubbyhole mailboxes, taking special pains with Addison's. Then he flipped through the stack of unfiled messages. "Nothing, sir."

"I'll be in the bar. Please page me if anything comes in." It was the third time in an hour that Addison had given the same instructions. He handed the clerk a ten-dollar bill and watched his dour features brighten considerably.

"Certainly, Mr. Addison," he replied with real sincerety.

But Addison was hardly satisfied. He scanned the broad Regency Hotel lobby with the angry frustration of a prisoner looking for a way out of his cell. He realized he should have called first, from Washington. He had half a minute to decide. The plane had been about to leave, and phoning would have cost a precious hour. So look what you've accomplished, he thought sourly. You've been cooling your heels in this hotel for three hours. The clock above the checkout desk read ten-thirty. Where the hell could Nancy have gone? he wondered for the hundredth time. At first he thought the message he was bringing back from Johns Hopkins was good news. Now he was not so sure.

He had started out waiting in his room. He was certain it would be only a few minutes until Nancy returned his call. Had her husband erased the message? It would not matter. She knew where to reach him. She would be at Bundy's office or home. Where else? He gave her twenty minutes, the length of a cab ride uptown, before telephoning Dr. Bundy.

The woman's voice was firm and correct. She had no idea when the doctor would be available. No, she did not know if he had kept his appointments for that day. Addison listened carefully. Then he made her repeat her message.

"Is this sort of behavior typical of Dr. Bundy?" Addison pressed.

"Only when he plays golf," the woman allowed. "But certainly not for an entire day. We've had a number of patients calling in, Mr. Addison. I wish there was more I could tell you."

"We got his message last night. It sounded important. He must have seen Miss Seymour. Doesn't he keep an appointment log?"

"I'm sure he does, Mr. Addison. But I'm just his answering service. You'll have to call his office in the morning."

Addison heard the ring of sympathetic concern behind the woman's professional tone. He could see no point in harassing her further.

The longer he waited, the stronger his feeling grew that neither Nancy nor Bundy were going to return his calls. He had turned his back for a moment and the earth had swallowed them up. All the way back he counted the minutes until he would see Nancy's eyes sparkle and hear her laugh. Now he felt cheated. The only way to have her, he was convinced, was to get her away from doctors. All doctors. Especially her husband. His mind flashed back to the small frozen animals inside Bendel's cloudy glass cages. They were just things that scientists poked and studied. Neither dead nor alive; just things. It made him angry. He did not care that NAC might have grasped some bit of technology that Johns Hopkins missed. Even with Bendel's photocopied notes bulging in his pocket, he suspected that they were all covering up, right to the end. He did not trust doctors, any of them.

Still, he thought, you may have done far better than you expected. The notes weighed as heavily as a bankroll on a Las Vegas tourist. He had his kernel of hard information.

Sam, the guinea pig, had been frozen alive. But Nancy Seymour was supposed to have a death certificate. Was that what Bendel had meant when he said there was a difference of degree? Could somebody move the starting line? At what point did the cryonic process begin? What did Stepp know that the Egyptian shamans who cut out the heart and liver with a sharp rock and bound the body in gauze didn't? Bundy might just have the answer.

Addison studied Bundy's darkened three-story town house. It stood out like a missing tooth on a block where most of the lights still shone. He knew it would be simple enough to enter, either through the front door or some unlatched window above the alley that provided a convenient fire-escape ladder. But there was always the possibility of an alarm, or worse, some light-sleeping housekeeper with a nervous trigger finger.

He walked up the steps and opened the outer door. A second, inner door was locked. He leaned on the buttons beneath Bundy's mailboxes. As he expected, nothing happened. The lock had a brass lip that overlapped the latch space. A credit card would not do. He took out his ring of half a dozen master keys. Suddenly a headlight cast his dark shadow across the brightly lit doorway. He flattened against the wall as a black-and-white police car cruised slowly past the building.

Addison held his breath until it turned the corner. He knew it would be only a few minutes until the cops repeated their route. There was no time to fumble with keys. He took off his raincoat and wrapped it over his fist. The trick, he recalled, was to pick a spot in the corner of the glass door, directly above the lock. He pushed away the fear of pain and shattered the glass.

The door buzzed. Addison froze for a moment. Then he shoved it open. No light went on. Nothing stirred.

"Hello," he shouted up the dark stairway. "Dr. Bundy?"

He found a light switch. Being able to see where he was going made him feel slightly less like a second-story man.

A phone began to ring somewhere down the long corridor. Addison found himself running toward the sound. He pushed open the door to the waiting room. The lit button on the receptionist's telephone pulsed like a tiny beacon. He snatched up the receiver.

"Dr. Bundy's office," was the first thing he thought to say.

"Bill Addison," the answer came in an irritated, high-pitched voice, "I know it's you. What took you so long?"

"Who is this?" Addison demanded. Then he noticed the thin ray of light under Bundy's office door. The phone clicked dead in his hand.

Addison moved quietly, touching the door so it swung open by its own weight. The light came from Bundy's desk lamp. The rest of the office was totally devastated. Every cabinet had been torn open. Files and books were strewn about like residue after a tornado. In that instant Addison knew with absolute clarity that he had made a mistake. He never should have left Nancy alone. He walked back into the reception room and called the police.

The 911 emergency number played a soothing selection of Mantovani while he waited for a connection. An old doctor and Nancy. What the hell does her apartment look like? he thought in a flash of urgency.

" . . . burglary. Burglary, the place was tossed," he told the police operator. "No, the doctor isn't around." He heard a click.

"Stay where you are, Mr. Addison. A squad car will be right over."

"Okay."

A click. A footstep. Addison slammed down the receiver and bolted for the front door. The noise had come from directly above him. Someone had been on the line. He stopped at the staircase. There's a burglar up there, he thought. Why the hell can't you have a gun when you need one? But he knew your name, just like he was expecting you.

"This is Addison," he shouted. "I'm coming up. I want to to talk to you."

"You called the police. You bastard, you." The voice was muffled by an upstairs door. It was a whine or a moan of disappointment—Addison could not tell for sure. But his instincts told him he had nothing more to fear.

"Don't get nervous. I'm coming up to talk." Addison made as much noise as he could climbing the stairs. It did not pay to surprise someone who might have a gun and an unhappy disposition. Only one bedroom door was closed. He pushed it open. A pair of lace curtains flapped in the breeze of a wide-open window. You jerk, he thought, crossing the room in two long strides. He caught sight of him halfway down the alley, just as he darted into the shadows. A moment later he was gone.

The sound of a siren drew closer. It was coming from the wrong direction. The cops would never see him. Addison stepped back from the window. You almost got him, he thought. No. He almost let you get him. Why did he wait so long to duck out? The answer was clear the moment Addison turned around. It was scrawled in bright red lipstick on the vanity mirror.

NANCY IN DANGER.
TIME SHORT. HELP.

The police were banging at the front door. Addison snatched a blanket off the bed and smeared the lipstick beyond reading. Then he answered the door.

Two cops stood shoulder to shoulder, eyeing him suspiciously. A second squad car had pulled up to cover the alley.

"You the guy who reported a burglary?" the bigger one asked. He rocked forward, close enough for Addison to feel a gentle rain of spittle as he spoke.

"Yes. You just missed him. He got out a window two minutes before you showed."

"Very interesting. Who the hell are you, the butler?" the cop snapped.

Addison handed him a business card. "I came over to see the doctor. Whoever tossed the place must have let me in."

"Maybe, Mr. Addison," he said politely enough to allow for the possibility that Addison might be telling the truth. "Now, let's see the damage."

Addison pointed the way to Bundy's office. The big cop pressed ahead, but the second one hung back. He studied Addison's card closely. "I'm Officer Kinski," he said. "He's Mulhern. This is a very classy card, raised lettering and all. So what does International Security, Inc., do for a living, Mr. Addison? You a private detective, or something? Haven't they got any doctors in Washington?"

Very reasonable questions to ask a man at the scene of a crime, Addison thought. But don't be in too much of a hurry. Whoever pulled this job knew you would be here too.

"Special protection, antiterrorist work, kidnapping prevention, a lot of seminars, that sort of thing. I was with the FBI for twelve years before I started the company."

"What about the doctor?"

"I came about a mutual friend."

Kinski shook his head, accepting the answer for the moment. He directed Addison into Bundy's office. Mulhern was just hanging up the phone.

"Midtown South is sending over a couple of detectives. We'll wait for them. Mr. Addison, you have a seat on that comfortable-looking sofa and tell us what you know about this mess." Mulhern gestured around the office, making a show of brushing a few loose folders off the corner of Bundy's desk to make room for his ample rump.

"I'll check out the rest of the house," Kinski said. "You said the burglar was upstairs, Mr. Addison?"

"Yes," Addison answered, barely listening. It was Mulhern's question that had grabbed his attention. What the hell *did* happen? he wondered. He studied the room with his own policeman's eye.

"It's supposed to look like a sloppy, amateur job," Addison ventured. "But I bet you don't find any jimmy marks on the doors or windows. You probably won't find anything missing, either."

"And just what makes you think all that?" Mulhern rubbed his jutting chin, indicating sufficient interest to keep listening.

Addison recalled his own warning.

"Gut feeling, that's all. This isn't the first break-in I've seen," he added quickly. "The IBM typewriter's still here. So is the Dictaphone. Even if it was only drugs he was after, he wouldn't have bothered wrecking the place."

"You never know. We see some pretty whacked-out junkies," Mulhern answered casually. But he crossed the office and stuck his head in the examining room.

"Damned if you ain't right. The drug cabinets are still locked. Did you happen to see that before we got here, Mr. Addison?"

"Let's cut the bullshit, Mulhern," Addison said angrily. "I'm a busy man. If you want to charge me with something, say so."

"Don't get sore, okay? To me, you don't look like the type

who'd do this kind of job. Not enough crazy in the eyes. You know what I mean? The rotten scumbags who do shit like this always squint, even if it's just a little bit. Besides, your clothes are too neat. Tearing up a joint like this, you'd have mussed your five-hundred-dollar suit. We friends again?" Mulhern smiled. "Now, what brought you here at eleven o'clock at night?"

"I came to get a line on Nancy Seymour. You know the name?"

"Sure. Who don't?"

A door slammed somewhere at the other end of the house.

"Jack, get down here," Kinski shouted.

Mulhern crossed the office with a quickness that belied his girth. His gun was halfway out of its holster.

"Come on." He motioned to Addison. "You first."

He did not have to ask. Addison was already two steps ahead of him. The shout had gone off in his head like an alarm siren. He could think of only one reason why Kinski was calling. The handwriting was on the wall, so to speak, he thought.

Kinski beckoned from the top of the basement stairs. They clattered after him all the way to the bottom, across a tiny furnace room to a dimly lit corner. Addison saw his old shoes first. The tops had been scuffed raw. His round little body sat propped up against a grimy oil burner. Kinski shone his flashlight on the face. There was a small red hole, like a Hindu caste mark, in the middle of his forehead.

"That's Bundy," Addison said. He knelt down beside the body and moved its head from side to side. Then he felt the singed, sticky underside where the bullet had entered.

"Hey, lay off the corpse," Mulhern snapped. "We pay a coroner for that kind of thing. You're not finished being a suspect."

Addison ignored the threat. One phone call would place him safely in Washington at the time of Bundy's murder. The stiffness of Bundy's neck and the yellow pallor of his skin were clear proof that he had been dead for at least a full day. Shot at close range with a small-caliber pistol and dragged here, Addison decided. He brushed the stubble of beard that had sprouted since Bundy's last shave. It was the only sign of untidiness he could find. The old man's tie was still perfectly straight and his collar rested neatly inside the lapels of his suit. Suddenly he was dead certain that he had been right. The police would find no sign of forced entry because Bundy knew his killer. Addison could read that much from the thin smile that lingered on the bloodless lips.

He saw the scrawl on the mirror. With Bundy's body at his feet, he had no further doubt of its truth or of its urgency.

Willie Garvin mingled with the crowd that had formed across the street. Mostly they just paused for a glance over the police barricade. A small hard core, with nothing better to do, hung around to wait out the action. Then the reporters began to arrive in their colorful vans. With brisk efficiency the crews set up their television cameras and light stands. The crowd quickly swelled to the limits of the sidewalk. Willie hoped the rain would hold off. The more people around, the safer he felt.

He only wished he was better dressed, and not quite so frightened. Then he would march across the street and bang on Bundy's front door. When a cop answered, he would demand to see Bill Addison. His lawyer—that's what I'd tell them, Willie decided. God knows he probably needs one by now. The fool. If only he'd given me a few more minutes. I know I could have found the package. All those reports; they had to be about Nancy. If only Addison hadn't bumbled in. No, that is not fair, he reprimanded himself. Nancy loves him. You have to trust him too. He'll do his best, whatever that might turn out to be.

The front door opened. Willie fought his way to the head of the crowd. Addison was taller than most. Willie was sure he would be able to see him, if just for a moment, between the bobbing heads that infuriated him by blocking his line of sight. I got here first, he wanted to shout. This is important to me. Let me see.

The stretcher-bearers led the way. The sight of a dead body worked like a jolt of electricity through the crowd. Ears perked and eyes strained. Perhaps another body would follow. But from then on it was just cops and reporters, coming and going. The crowd began to lose interest. Come on, Willie thought, stamping his feet to keep warm, I can't stand here all damned night. Then he saw Addision silhouetted by the foyer light. He could clearly see that he was not wearing handcuffs.

"Thank God," he said loud enough for the woman next to him to turn around. Now he would have to go uptown and wait a little longer, but that was not so bad. He knew that soon enough they would both be free.

21

Nancy felt the coldness creep up from her toes. She bundled her arms close to her sides. All at once she was wide-awake and clearheaded. The cold was bracing as a splash of fresh water. She lay still for a moment, savoring the sensation. Her body told her that the drugs had run their course. She opened her eyes. Darkness gave way to hazy shapes as she gradually grew accustomed to the dim moonlight through the window beside her bed. Then all her senses began to work together. She remembered Stepp's dark eyes and the pain when he touched her neck. "That bastard," she hissed, stretching her muscles. She could not move. Leather straps bound her tight to the bed.

The wave of shock passed as she quickly realized the bed was only a narrow stretcher. The straps were simply to keep her from rolling off. She slid one arm free, then the other. The cold, the faint distant hum of machinery, and the general outline of her small room all came together. They took you back to NAC, she thought. She was sure that if she could turn around to the window she would see a vast parking lot surrounded by landscaped lawns and distant hills. NAC, she allowed sarcastically, was an excellent suburban corporate citizen. She was angry, but as deadly calm as she could remember. Now, Nancy, she told herself, it's time to go home.

Getting free of the stretcher was a small problem, like squirming out of a sleeping bag. Her feet felt cold on the bare floor. She quickly donned the slippers and bathrobe folded over the room's only chair. Her eyes were drawn to the window. In the distance she could make out the glow of lights from the highway. It was fifty-two miles back to New York. That part was a detail. She sensed that her real problem was going to be getting past the front gate of NAC. A strong feeling warned her to trust no one. She knew how hospitals worked and she bitterly remembered Dr. Latimer. They would all try to stop her.

She heard footsteps in the hall and froze with her ear flush to the door. Two pairs of feet and a piece of rolling equipment drew closer. Nancy held her breath. She could hear their voices through the thin wooden door. The sounds drew abreast of her, then gradually began to fade as the men continued down the hallway. Nancy waited until she could hear nothing at all before opening the door a crack. She looked both ways. The corridor was empty. There were no signs posted, but she knew just where she was. Her mind shot back almost a year. She could still vividly recall the pain of the military fever in her knees and ankles as she suffered to keep pace with Amos Stepp's brisk strides.

"Patient Care is down that way, Nancy," Stepp told her. "We've got the whole west wing, everything past that door. Spartan, but clean. We're no plush hospital. We're a research center. Right now we use the rooms for volunteer drug testing. But all that will change soon enough. We'll see to that, won't we?"

You listened to that snake charmer, Nancy rebuked herself. You were sick and he had all the answers. And you trusted your husband, the doctor. Now the money grubbers are afraid of some bad publicity. You've become an embarrassment. They'll find some good medical excuse to keep you out of sight. Even if that means another stint in the tank while they figure out what went wrong. How much did they have to pay the noble Dr. Bundy to drop out of sight? She pushed her anger aside. There would be time enough for that later, she decided. She padded silently toward the elevator, just past the patient-care wing. A right turn, she recalled, would lead to the cryonic-research laboratories. She pictured Stepp and her husband hunched over a bubbling caldron. Brewing up another batch of sleazy tricks, she thought. After I get back to the station with this story, they will be lucky to find a rat to freeze.

What story? Nancy fumed with frustration. A brilliant doctor who has already saved your life once says you need help, and you say you don't. She pictured the lead story line: "Ungrateful patient battles Nobel Prize winner." Very appealing. They'll laugh you off the air. You're so turned around that you don't even trust your own instincts, she thought. No wonder NBC sent you packing.

Nancy stopped short of pushing the elevator button. Everything had gone too smoothly. Unlocked doors; empty hallways. It was not what she had expected. Not after the sting of Dr. Latimer's needle and the painful touch of Stepp's hand. If Stepp lets you walk out of here, she thought, then you've misread everything. She pushed the elevator button. A red light above her head immediately began to blink. The alarm was almost a relief. Anything was better than being so completely wrong. A door opened halfway down the hall. A large, very blond young man in a starched white medical jacket rubbed the sleep from his eyes as he walked towards her. "Miss Seymour, what are you doing up at this hour?" he said in a scolding tone. "Let's go back to your room."

"I was looking for a cigarette machine," Nancy shot back. "You go lie on that damned hard stretcher. I expect to find a decent bed in my room when I return. Where are my husband and Dr. Stepp?"

"My instructions are . . ." He continued lamely.

Nancy sensed her advantage. "Who the devil are you?" she demanded.

"Jerry Muller. I'm the night duty clerk. I'll call Dr. Victor for you. I know he's on the premises someplace. I'm sure he'll straighten out everything. I didn't know about the stretcher. They just brought you in. I thought . . ."

"Muller, I suggest you find those other two who were making all the racket and have them locate a bed for me. Now, where is a cigarette machine? Surely you've got one tucked away in this enormous building." Nancy could see her petulance was getting results. Muller did not know which way to jump first.

"Look, Miss Seymour, I'll find you some cigarettes and a bed. But while you're in this wing, I'm responsible for you. Don't make my life tough. I was told you weren't supposed to be walking around. Why don't you wait in my office? I'll get you a bed and I'll get Dr. Victor."

"First get the bed," Nancy demanded.

"Okay, okay. Don't get excited. Sit down in the office. And please don't wander off. You can't go anyplace anyway. This floor is sealed. You ought to know that."

"The last time I was here I got some decent treatment. Why is the floor sealed?"

"Look, just wait in there. I'll be right back." He gestured toward the open door and started off in the opposite direction. They don't hire them for their brains, Nancy thought.

She headed for the door Muller had indicated. She paused for a quick glance inside, with absolutely no thought of sitting down to wait. She had been expecting a cubbyhole with a rumpled cot and some empty beer cans in the trash basket. What she saw stopped her cold. An entire wall was formed of closed-circuit-television screens. Below each screen was a designation of the area being scanned. Muller's desk was a control panel of lights and switches and keys. Dozens of keys. Each sector of the control panel was key-operated. An additional key ring hung from the back of his chair.

Nancy sat down at the panel like a driver getting behind the wheel for the first time. It began to make sense to her as soon as she recognized the similarities to a television-studio console. The large black dials controlled the cameras' direction while the levers were used for close-ups. She picked a screen marked "West Delivery Entrance" for a quick experiment. The camera panned back from the door, showing a length of empty hallway. She checked the entire array until she located Muller. He was talking in animated gestures to two other white-coated men. Nancy zeroed in for a tight close-up of their faces. For a moment she had the pleasant sensation of manipulating a cast of players. She thought she might enjoy Muller's job, for a little while at least. What's the matter with you? she almost burst out. Now you've got a real chance to get out of here. Her eyes took in the entire control panel. Muller's face came in on the screen marked "Patient Care—4th Floor."

She knew she had to keep a watchful eye on him, even while she checked the wall-mounted diagram of the alarm system.

She flipped the switch marked "Elevator" and the one system beside it, "Stairway." The red lights on the diagram turned to green.

Muller and the two others had disappeared from her screen. She located them on the one below, unlocking a supply-room door. I've got at least five minutes, she estimated. He hasn't even started looking for my cigarettes yet.

A trench coat was hanging on the back of the door. It was twice Nancy's size, but she wrapped it around herself and tightened the belt. She paused at the doorway for a moment to be sure. The exit light over the stairway door shone like a beacon. It's safer than the elevator, she decided.

The cameras could be avoided on the stairs, but not in the elevators. It seemed so clear. She could walk right out of NAC. But something distracted her, like a light tap on the shoulder or the uncomfortable feeling of a stranger's gaze on the back of the neck. Her eyes swung around to the television monitors. Amos Stepp was staring out of the center screen.

Nancy recoiled like she had been slapped. Then she forced herself to look again. He was in an elevator, and very angry. His heavy lips flapped feverishly, baring his teeth as he spoke. The screen was labeled "North Wing," but that meant nothing to her. She strained to keep one eye on Stepp while she checked the floor-plan diagram. Then he moved aside and Nancy could see her husband. He appeared equally angry, standing cheek by jowl and shaking a finger in Stepp's face. She wished she could hear what they were saying. The elevator door slid open. For a moment she could see both their backs. She had no intention of waiting for more.

The stairway door opened quietly. Nancy savored the cool, dankish draft that wafted up. The dimness honed her fine edge of excitement. Yet she felt almost foolish at the same time, like a petulant schoolgirl intent on being difficult. A passing impulse warned her to go back, to listen to her husband and her doctor. To hell with them both, she thought. Trust yourself.

She was two landings down when she heard the first shouts. It was Muller.

"Miss Seymour, where are you? Please come back. There's no place you can go."

"Lady, where the hell are you. We ain't going to hurt you," said a second voice.

Nancy moved as quietly as she could, one step at a time. The stairway door opened above her. She pressed herself into the shadows.

"Jerry, you dumb bastard. You left her in the fucking control room. She threw the switches. The elevator, everything is workin'. Get the alarms back on before Stepp nails your ass to the barn door."

"Miss Seymour? You down there?"

The calls were growing frantic. Nancy held her breath. The door was still open. She was afraid they would hear her heart pounding.

"Jerry, are the alarms reset, dammit?" the one at the doorway asked. "Keep your eyes on the screens. She's got to surface. Open the intercoms if you spot anything. I'll get a flashlight and check the stairs. Phil, you look in every room on the floor. If we're real lucky, maybe she's so doped up she wandered off and nodded out someplace."

Stuff it, Nancy thought. Go get your goddamned flashlight. The door above clicked shut. You've only got a few seconds, she realized. He'll be right back and the alarms will be reset. She ran for the third-floor exit. She could not chance going farther. The light above the door turned red the moment it slammed shut behind her. She spun around to try the knob. It was locked. The building was sealed. For a moment she did not know which way to run.

She started down the corridor, pausing to catch her breath. It was surely the same building, but the third floor had almost nothing in common with the patient-care wing. The cold tile floors had been replaced by deep pile carpeting. The walls were paneled in rich wood. It was a soft, comfortable place where executives padded quietly during the day. But Nancy knew that even here the cameras stood silent guard. The elevators were dead and the stairs locked. There was no way off the floor. They'll find you, it's only a matter of minutes, she thought. "Why?" she shouted in rage. "Why are you running? Why are you so afraid? They saved your life."

Reason did not work. Nancy's instincts took over. She was being hunted. Every living creature has a sense of danger, and the pounding of her heart told her to flee. She ran, pausing only to try the doors she passed, not caring where they led. The whole building was a trap. She knew she was going in a great circle. She would wind up back at the same stairway. And they would be waiting for her. Who?

A knob turned. She flung open the heavy wooden door and fumbled for a light switch. It was a large, gracious office with a glass table for a desk and potted palms beside the windows. The soft armchairs called out to the aches in her body. She wanted to lie down and close her eyes. You can't, a voice inside her head warned her. Not yet. She closed the door and turned the lock. For a moment the dull thud of a bolt falling made her feel safe and secure.

The phone on the glass table caught her eye like a lifeline in a choppy sea. She snatched it up and punched out a memorized number.

"This is a recording . . . 203 . . . Please dial 1 and your area code before—"

"Goddammit," she shouted in frustration. She had completely forgotten that she was in Connecticut. More seconds wasted. She redialed, listened to the sounds outside her door grow louder and clearer.

"Nancy, we know you're in there." It was Victor's pleading voice. "Please come out."

The phone rang and rang.

"Nancy, we just want to help you."

"Regency Hotel, good evening," they answered at last.

"Mr. Addison," Nancy whispered.

The rattling outside grew sharper, the buzzing voices more impatient and angrier.

"Please speak up. I can't hear you."

"Mr. Addison, Bill Addison," Nancy shouted. She no longer cared if the people outside heard her.

"One moment, please. I'll connect you."

Nancy had never known that a moment could take so long.

"Well, get the key, you idiot." She heard Amos Stepp's rude bark. "Now."

"I'm sorry. Mr. Addison's room does not answer."

"Give him a message. Please. It's very important. This is Nancy Seymour. I'm at NAC. He has to come get me. Please, as soon as he comes in."

"I'll make sure he gets it," the unflappable voice responded.

Nancy hung up just as the office door began to open. She saw five of them. Stepp, the orderlies, and her husband.

"John, for God's sake, what is going on? Why are you treating me like a prisoner?"

Victor turned his eyes to avoid her stare.

"Now will you believe me, John?" Stepp said coldly. "We have a problem that must be addressed."

Nancy had no doubt he was referring to her. Victor shook his head in sad agreement. Then she saw the hypodermic needle in Muller's hand. Someone grabbed her from behind. She closed her eyes and kicked wildly.

"You bastards," she screamed. "Let me go!"

The pain in her arm was no more than a mosquito bite, but the fight drained out of her like a bag of sand falling through a trapdoor.

John Victor summoned up his years of professional detachment. It was a trick that he had picked up very early on in medical school. You can only suffer along with your patients on an intellectual level. If personal concern ever begins to affect judgment, that is time to turn the case over to someone less involved. So a doctor with decent common sense never operates on a member of his own family. Until Victor watched his wife being stuffed like a sausage into a straitjacket, the matter had never much concerned him. He was not one to lavish emotions on things depressing. His few patients suffered alone. But Nancy was his wife and it made him angry that anything belonging to him would be handled with so little respect. He would never allow it to happen to one of his cars.

"Be careful, will you, Muller? Don't make that thing so damned tight," he snapped.

Muller smiled, feigning a sheepish remorse. "No sir, Dr. Victor," he said. "We'll be sure she's nice and comfy for the trip."

Then he lifted Nancy into a wheelchair. A moment later they were gone out the office door. Victor started after them.

"Hold it. Just one minute," he shouted. Muller glanced back from the elevator area. The cold glint in his eyes spoke volumes. Victor could no longer deny to himself what he had secretly known all along. There was only one logical reason for bringing Nancy back to NAC. They are going to kill her, he thought, but his feet were riveted of the ground.

"Muller, I won't permit this," he said, a bit louder. Muller ignored him. He maneuvered Nancy's wheelchair into the elevator and waved as the door closed behind them. Victor turned to Stepp. His voice dropped to a hoarse whisper. "Amos, I won't allow any real harm to come to Nancy. My mind is made up."

"Come along, John," Stepp said agreeably, guiding him toward the elevators. "We've still got a few details to tidy up before we can join them. But first I think you need a breath of fresh air. This has been a most trying evening and you're simply not thinking straight."

Victor was not exactly sure that Stepp had answered him, but he let himself be encouraged.

"We've made enough money, Amos. They'll never find it all," he said eagerly. "Forget Nancy. We can get out now, while the others are still here to hold the bag for us."

"Money? Certainly we've made money. We deserve to make money. Our work requires money. But now that you've finally gotten your hands on all that money, John, don't you find you want something more?"

The question pierced Victor like a knife. How do you walk away clean? How can you remain forever the eminent Dr. John Victor? He had basked in respect like a dungeon prisoner let into the sunshine. For the first time in his memory he overheard people quote him. He was listened to. Respected. Losing that was a grim prospect. Stepp was right; money could not buy it back. He cringed at the sour memory of the acquaintances who had once laughed at him or avoided him for fear he would put the arm on them or bore them senseless. He hated those people. Success had been his sweet revenge. He followed Stepp across the brightly lit, deserted lobby, still conjuring for some way to hang on to it.

"She made a call, Amos. Someone knows she is here."

"That is exactly why we must take her elsewhere, John. You know perfectly well who she would call." Stepp's lips curled into a lascivious leer. "Your rival, Mr. Addison. Come, now, John, don't look so shocked at the mention of his name. He's been screwing her—"

"That's enough, Amos," Victor cut in. "She wouldn't have had the chance to make a call if you'd given her a standard anesthetic instead of some yoga rabbit punch."

Stepp bristled, just the way Victor hoped he would. His small, round body tilted forward as stubby legs quick-marched out the front door. Victor followed into the gusty night air. The clouds had been blown away. He saw the stars, brighter than they ever were in the city. Then his eyes dropped across the wide concrete pavilion, to the ambulance that was just pulling away. Stepp saw it too.

"John, I'm sorry. We both talk too much. I know this must be especially difficult for you. From here on things will go very smoothly. You have no further need for concern. I promise."

Stepp's sympathy shocked Victor more than the anger he had expected. It was an answer, just as surely as the direction the ambulance had taken when it left the parking lot. Anger could have been argued. It spoke to greed, and that was an ache Victor understood well enough. But sympathy, Victor thought, was the sound of a door being slammed in his face.

"God, Amos," he exploded in disgust. "You must think I'm an idiot. You seduced me, just as sure as Addison seduced my wife. We could make a fortune, you whispered like a snake in my ear. And with the right lawyers covering our trail, it would all be perfectly legal. Well, we've come a long way since then and we've left 'legal' far behind. I have to admit, Amos, that once I was in, I started to enjoy it. The money. The power. Working all day and then watching it unfold on television at night. All the letters and the phone calls and the bribes, all begging for help. I never imagined that so many people craved immortality. But, Amos, it was always just a scam. Christ, I've been bullshitting people all my life. How the hell do you think I ever got through medical school? All you did was take me out of the bush leagues. At least I never got hooked on my own fantasies."

"Fantasy? You ignorant man," Stepp scolded. "Cryonic suspension is the dream of mankind. Do you think we could have come this far if my work were invalid? All you do is prance around in your custom-made suits and open your mouth when a microphone pops up. Meanwhile, every biological laboratory in the country is scrutinizing my work. Or did you think the world would simply take your word that cryonic suspension worked? The DSMO body-wash concept alone should earn me another Noble Prize nomination. The tissues can be protected against extreme cold. And the polymer body seal for skin protection—"

"I know," Victor cut in. "You could go on for hours telling me how brilliant you are. Well, if you've got all the bugs out of cryonic suspension, Amos, how come we're going out to the farm to start murdering my wife?"

22

Nancy Seymour is in danger. A burglar left me a message on Bundy's mirror, Addison thought. The cops would have loved that one. He pushed open the paint-chipped green door. The gray dawn light was bright enough to make him squint. The street was freshly washed and even the garbage-can lids seemed tightly secure. Compared with the precinct's rank odors of cigar smoke and sweat, the narrow, empty street was pristine as a national park. Addison shook his head and stretched his muscles. He ached all over.

Everybody was polite as hell, he recalled. And every damned thing took hours. Watching the cops shuffle papers was a slow-motion act. But he knew he was one of the lucky ones.

"FBI man," somebody had whispered when the cops led him into the station. They did not even bother with the booking desk. Right up stairs to the detectives' squad room. They started him out on coffee and doughnuts. Most of the people who were waiting when he arrived were still waiting when he left. He had not actually seen their faces. The quick walk through the station house allowed only a moment for impressions. Everybody was slumped on benches, like the crowd that sifts into a Central American railroad depot when it is raining and the last train of the night is long gone. He was glad to be rid of the place.

Addison walked until he found an all-night diner. His body was tired, but his brain churned with worry. NAC had big money on the line. They were not about to admit that anything might be wrong with their cryonic process. Corporations were just people. He knew well enough that they were capable of nasty things when threatened. But logic kept tugging at his sleeve. Much as he wanted to, he could not find the thread that bound NAC to Bundy's rigid body. It certainly wasn't that they lacked the means, or even the will, just the clear reason. Addison remembered Bundy's voice on the telephone-answering tape. It was important, he had said ominously, or so it seemed now. But what could Bundy know that Johns Hopkins did not? Bendel was still alive and well, and only skeptical.

Addison knew he needed time. Perhaps only hours, but perhaps days, to sort it all out. He felt like a computer that was about to overload. Garbage in; garbage out. Did Nancy see the murderer? Was she in Bundy's office when it happened? Did he kill her too? No. She's in danger, not dead. The burglar told you, remember? You're standing waist-deep in shit and sinking fast, Addison thought in disgust. You know nothing. For a moment he thought he should have told the police. At least he would not be working alone. Or find her sleazy son-of-a-bitch husband, he thought, and beat the hell out of him until he comes up with some answers. Both reckless thoughts, he knew very well, would have gotten anyone who worked for him fired on the spot. He sensed that a cup of coffee was being set in front of him and instinctively reached out for the cream pitcher. Someone slid it across the glistening Formica counter into his open hand. He glanced up at the smiling face two stools over.

"You want the sugar too?" he said in a soft, high-pitched twang.

"You going to slip me a message under the napkin?" Addison's hand shot out, grasping the thin man's rumpled lapel. He yanked him forward until their faces were nearly touching. The thin man's eyes widened in fear and surprise. Then Addison's hand gradually relaxed as it dawned on him just who had found whom. "Who the hell are you?" he demanded. "What were you doing at Bundy's place?"

"Willie Garvin," he responded in a trembling voice. "I . . . I'm a friend of Nancy Seymour. Can we go someplace safe?"

Addison had a sudden urge to fling the wisp of a man through the diner's plate-glass window. Just the sound of her name had brought back the pain of Nancy's nightmare scream. He had hit the right nerve. Addison had to listen.

"Hey, mister," he heard the counterman's voice over his shoulder. "This faggot bothering you? I'll throw him the hell outta here."

Willie sat up straight on his stool, summoning up his dignity from beneath a three-day growth of stubbly beard and an overcoat two sizes too large. "You leave us alone," he said to the burly counterman. "We're talking business."

"You don't say?" the counterman minced.

Willie's lip quivered. It angered Addison that the shabby, middle-aged waif seemed so natural a victim. As though he had hung out a sign, a lightning rod for anyone's aimless hostility, even his own.

"You heard him," Addision said to the counterman. "Piss off."

Willie's face brightened. He ran a hand through his closely cropped grayish hair and turned down his collar like a man getting himself ready for a big interview.

"You do believe me, Mr. Addison? Nancy is in danger. I'm sure of it. Come on. I know a place where we can go. I'm not safe here," Willie said in one gasp of breath.

"Willie, so far all I know is that maybe you're a second-story man and maybe you're a murderer," Addision said patiently. "And you like to write on mirrors."

"I knew your name. I knew you were coming to Bundy's office. Isn't that enough?" Willie's excitement grew.

Addison knew that his name and face could have been gleaned from any one of dozens of articles or television appearances relating to his business. Nancy was a public figure, even before the cryonic suspension. Perhaps this man had seen us together, he thought, or picked up some snippet of gossip. But it was not a simple money scam. He saw that much from the fear and intensity in Willie's narrow slit eyes. But that still doesn't rule out loony, he reasoned.

"You mean to tell me that you actually knew Nancy?" he prodded Willie.

"Yes." Willie's shrill reply brought two other customers out of their newspapers. He immediately dropped to a whisper. "We've got to get out of here. They're all looking at us. Sitting here, people can even see us from the street."

"I'd say that would be far worse for my reputation than yours."

"You're all such snobs. I'm in disguise. My life is in danger every minute, just like Nancy. I must save her. I love her. She's mine."

Addison watched the little man shake with indignation. "Are you crazy?" he asked sincerely. "Look, Willie, I haven't got time or patience for any bullshit."

"Oh, God!" Willie moaned. "I know I must sound like a madman, and look it too. Please, believe me, I love Nancy. I can help her, but I need your help. They'll kill me if—"

Addison held up his hand to cut him off. It took him only a moment to review his alternatives. Then his eyes came back to Willie. My best bet, he thought bleakly.

"Okay, Willie, I know you're in a big hurry. I only need two quick answers before we run out to save your ass and the rest of the world. Did you kill Bundy?"

Willie's face turned ashen white. For a moment Addison feared he might throw up.

"He's dead?" Willie whispered. "That's why you said murderer. . . . They killed him. My God . . ."

"All right, I'll buy that. You'd have gotten a hernia dragging that body."

"The same people are after me. I'm sure of it. He was treating Nancy. He was her friend."

"Willie, I know all that. What do you know about cryonic suspension?"

Willie bounced off his stool. An elfin grin spread across his face as he took Addison by the arm and led him out the front door. "Absolutely everything," he whispered in Addison's ear. "Absolutely everything."

"It's mine. I bought it. Do you like it, Bill?" Willie chirped.

Addison glanced around the interior of the battered old car. The stick of air freshener dangling from the rearview mirror swayed like a plumb bob as Willie veered and swerved to avoid Third Avenue's cavernous potholes. Horns blasted on all sides.

"It's a real beauty. Slow down before you hit something and spoil the finish."

"You don't like her." Willie's voice turned to a pout. "She isn't pretty, like Nancy. But she can sure go like hell. Besides, I risked my life buying her. Doesn't that count for anything? They could have traced the registration. But I knew we'd need a dependable car; not flashy, just dependable."

"Willie, what is all this crap about people chasing you?" Addison asked. Who in the world but another crazy bastard like me would have anything to do with you? he thought. "Now, you've got about five minutes until we get to the Regency to come up with some straight answers about cryonics and the other shit you've been handing me. Otherwise, Willie, I'm going to turn you inside out just for wasting my time."

Willie slammed on his brakes. The car immediately behind them screeched to a halt. Then Addison heard the crash of metal and glass. It came like light bulbs bursting on concrete, all the way down the lane.

"You dumb bastard," he shouted in Willie's ear. Willie turned off the engine. He slammed the wheel with his fist as tears streamed down his cheeks.

"Go away!" he screamed. "Leave me alone. I should never have trusted you. I'll save Nancy myself. I did a terrible thing and now you're making me pay for it."

Addison shot a glance over his shoulder. The sight of people pouring out of their cars, yelling curses and swapping licenses, sped his decision. He knew that any second the crowd would start to converge on Willie. If it's a bluff, then, damn you, it worked, he thought. The notion of a second run-in with the police was even less attractive than Willie's histrionics. The light turned green.

"Okay, Willie, I trust you. Now, let's get the hell out of here."

Willie wiped his tears away with slow, measured movements. "You really trust me? You won't threaten me, or ask any more questions about the others . . . or the terrible things I—"

"No. Now, move it before the cops show up."

The car leaped forward. There was almost no traffic ahead of them, and in a moment the accident was far behind.

Addison blew a long sigh of relief. "You can tell me about

cryonics, can't you, Willie?" he asked quietly, not wanting to precipitate another demolition derby.

Willie burst into a high-pitched giggle. "Cyronics? Sure, Bill. Cryonics is a big joke."

Brilliant, Addison thought. Bendel showes me around a three-hundred-million dollar research facility and Willie says it's a lot of crap. But Addision knew there was more to it. He was certain that Willie had something that Bendel and all the other white-jacketed rat runners lacked. He cared about Nancy. Why? Addison wondered.

Willie slid the car into the doorman's spot directly in front of the Regency's canopy.

"What are we going to do here, Bill?" he asked nervously. "We haven't got any time to waste."

"Willie, I'm going to take a shave and change my shirt. Whatever you will or won't tell me will certainly hold for another fifteen minutes. You can wait here if you want. Or go your own way."

Addison got out of the car without waiting for an answer. Willie watched him until he disappeared through the revolving front door. All the while his foot trembled just above the accelerator pedal. His instincts warned him to flee. Did they really kill Bundy? he wondered fitfully. He turned on the radio, hoping for some confirmation, or better still, no confirmation at all. If they would kill an important man like Bundy, he thought, they'll step on me like a cockroach. You can't do anything alone, and Bill Addison is not going to help you. He doesn't trust you. He thinks you're weird. Willie chuckled. God knows, the police won't help you either. That thought just churned more fear in his stomach. He began to chant aloud, rapping his knuckles on the steering wheel in tempo with his verse:

They'll bash my bones
And crush my head,
They'll freeze my ass
In nitrogen gas. . . .
What ails you, Willie?
It don't matter a lot.
When you get thawed out,
You'll be red-hot.
A superstar. . . .

He burst out laughing, with tears streaming down his cheeks.

"I love her," he bellowed at the doorman who had come out from under his protective canopy. "Why can't Bill trust me? Simple trust is all I want."

"Get this shit heap the hell outta my spot before I call the cops," the doorman snarled. He approached the car until he was close enough to get a good look at Willie's face. Then he drew back to a safe distance, as though something in Willie's bedraggled appearance might be contagious. "I don't care about your problems, buddy," he shouted. "Just get the hell out of here."

Willie heard the ring of a prudent suggestion through the man's threatening tone.

"Keep your fucking parking spot," he answered just loud enough to make sure he was heard over the revving of his engine. He had barely started to roll when he slammed on his brakes.

"Willie . . . hold it!" Addison shouted as he burst out of the revolving door. But it was not the call that had brought Willie to a dead stop. He turned up the volume of the radio and held his breath as though that were enough to bring the traffic's racket to an instant stop.

Addison jumped in beside him. "Willie, Nancy called me—" he began.

Willie waved him silent, his ear cocked to the radio. Addison, too, found himself listening for a moment. The station began to broadcast a traffic report.

"Damn!" Willie snapped. "It was Nancy. I'm sure they said something about Nancy."

"Listen to me, you idiot," Addison insisted. "I just got a message from Nancy. She called me from NAC. Now, if you want to do something, drive me the hell up there."

Willie shook his head like a man in a trance. "What did she say?" he asked numbly.

"Just what I told you. It was a message. I didn't talk to her. What are waiting for? Do you know how to get there?"

"Yes, I remember," Willie whispered. He wheeled the car around the Park Avenue island. Addison's attention was fixed on the slip of paper clenched in his fist. He read the message again, vainly trying to bring life to a few simple words: "I'm at NAC. Come as soon as you can. Nancy."

He could not even be sure that the words were exactly hers
and not some off hand interpretation scribbled by a bored
switchboard operator. But what concerned him most was that
the message was almost twelve hours old. He had immediately called her home. There was no answer.

"I told you so," Willie chirped in a tone so gleeful that it
jangled Addison's nerves. "They've got her."

"Who the hell has got her?" Addison asked, more irritated
than curious.

"Stepp, you fool. Stepp, her husband, that slimy bastard.
Maybe Kholer, who knows the others? The Cryonics Crazies,
we used to call them. . . ." Willie shot a hand to his mouth,
stemming his excited flow of words. But he had said enough.
Even paranoiacs have enemies, Addison thought. He could
see that Willie's fear was thick enough to hit with a stick.

"They are the people who are after you, too. Willie, I can
protect you. All you've got to do is level with me. Why is Dr.
Stepp after you?"

Addison patiently watched Willie's eyes dart between him
and the traffic. It was an old story that he had seen many
times before. Whom does the frightened witness trust the
least?

"We'll just get her out of there, Bill. Whatever they're doing to her. Whatever they tell us. We won't believe a word of
it. We'll just get her out of that damned NAC place. Then I'll
tell you everything. It's Nancy I want to save. I don't care
about myself."

Willie's voice was so full of pleading misery that Addison
was tempted to take him at his word. I'll buy this much, he
thought: anybody so down-and-out seedy couldn't give much
of a damn about himself.

"All right, Willie." Addison blew out a conciliatory sigh.
"We'll do it your way. God knows I've got no more use for
those doctors than you have. But what the hell are we saving
her from?"

"Shut up! Shut up!" Willie shouted.

For an instant Addison felt a surge of anger. Then he realized what Willie was doing and he turned his full attention
to the blaring radio.

. . . top story of the hour. Nancy Seymour has been returned to cryonic suspension. The former NBC news re-

porter was admitted to Bellevue Hospital last night following a severe attack of military fever, the disease that was thought to have been cured. Sources at North American Chemicals' cryonics division report that fears for her life necessitated a return to the facility while the tests were being evaluated. Sources report that Miss Seymour was in critical condition when taken from Bellevue to NAC's cryonic facility. . . . We will bring you a full report later in the hour. In a related story, her family physician was killed during a burglary of his office at—

Addison snapped off the radio. Willie's voice could have come from inside his own head: "You can bet your ass it's a related story, Bill."

We've got them surrounded, Addison mused, staring at the sprawling white building that dominated the horizon. Willie's negotiating a series of back country roads to save five minutes had not been lost on him. He watched while Willie maneuvered his car into a far corner of the lot, well out of sight of the main entrance of the building.

"Do we walk right up the steps and kick in the front door?" Addison asked, fully expecting the shocked reaction that flashed across Willie's face.

"Are you crazy? The place is crawling with security guards. They wouldn't let us anywhere near the cryonic labs. I know another way."

"I figured you would. You worked here, Willie. Was that when Nancy was here?"

A shake of the head was his only answer. Willie started off at a lope across the up-sloping lawn.

"Hurry up, Bill," he hissed over his shoulder. "The day shift will start showing up in half an hour and the place will be mobbed."

"Afraid you'll run into somebody you know?" Addison asked, venting his growing impatience. He did not like being fed scraps when he could smell the aroma of a banquet.

Willie bolted toward the trees that bordered the parking lot. Addison was surprised by his speed and agility. His long overcoat trailed out behind him like a cape in the breeze. A moment later he had disappeared into the heavy foliage. Addison caught up with him at the beginning of a narrow path.

A few steps had carried them completely out of sight of the corporate park. Willie slowed to a brisk walk. Addison judged their direction to be generally following the contour of the building. It was much larger than he had suspected from first glance or his last visit. When he tried to recall that visit, it seemed like a lifetime had passed. The memory churned inside him and made him angry for no reason he could clearly define.

Willie stopped suddenly. "Right through here," he announced.

To Addison's eye he seemed to be pointing at a thorny bush. Willie swept the foliage aside. They were almost flush against the building's white-brick wall. The trees had been cut back to accommodate a small gray concrete, pipe-railed slab, like a miniature patio in the middle of nowhere. Framed by a series of propane tanks, it took up almost the entire clearing. The matching gray door, without a knob or lock, appeared as functional as a window in the back of an elevator.

Willie broke into a grin. "It's a fire exit. I used to sneak out on my breaks. Practically nobody knows it's here."

"What the hell good is a fire exit that doesn't go anyplace?"

Willie shrugged. "So the architect screwed up. At least the door opens. I've heard of fire exits where people are trapped because—"

"Okay. It's a great fire exit. How do we get in?"

Without another word Willie jumped the two feet up to the slab. He studied the door with the exaggerated gestures of a magician setting up a card trick. Stripping off his bulky overcoat, he tossed it into the woods.

"Are you going to rip it off the hinges, Willie?" Addison asked impatiently.

"Don't be foolish," Willie responded in earnest. Then, bracing himself against the door for balance, he gingerly climbed atop the railing. His free hand groped the ledge above the door.

"Nothing changes," he said with a broad grin. When he jumped off the railing he was holding a long tube, flattened at the end like a slim shoehorn. "We used to come out here to deal drugs and smoke a little reefer. This is how we got back inside."

He slid the wide end of the improvised tool into the

doorjamb and bent it back slightly. Then he yanked and the door popped open a crack.

"Quick, hold it Bill," he said.

Addison caught the door with his fingertips while Willie straightened the tube and replaced it on the door ledge.

"A lot of my friends count on that little gizmo," he said by way of an explanation.

The impatient snap of Stepp's voice brought Victor scurrying out of the bathroom wrapped only in a large NAC-logo towel. Droplets of water flicked from his freshly washed hair darkened the deep beige carpeting around his feet. He glanced up from the puddle, across the expanse of the office, at Stepp sitting complacent as a fat frog behind his fortress of a desk. The thought crossed his mind that he had never had an office with a full bathroom and well-stocked bar. He found the thought depressing and began to pick at the dried bits of shaving cream that still adhered to his cheeks and neck. He was embarrassed. He was at least ten years Stepp's junior, but the night's work had left hardly a trace of wear on the older man's pink cheeks or the razor-sharp crease of his impeccable dark suit. Why isn't he frightened? Victor wondered.

"Well, get dressed, John," Stepp urged. "You can't meet the press in your bare ass. Tends to make a bad impression."

Victor had been told the press would be coming. He had never agreed to it. But he had to admit that Stepp had warned him well in advance. It was a part of the plan that struck him as just a touch too arrogant. Stepp called it boldness.

"All right, Amos, I guess I'll be ready. Once more the grieving husband. I'm damned sick of it. I can hardly keep my eyes open as it is," Victor found himself complaining. It felt good. "I've been up all night. Why the hell did we have to rush back here right this minute? We could have stalled for another day. God, I half-expect Addison to come bashing down the door."

"Nitwit." Stepp sighed heavily. "We were never supposed to have left. As for Addison, let him come. He can see what everybody else sees. Now, behave yourself, John, and I'll give you some very good news. We came back today because I've decided that tonight is the night we go out of business."

Victor felt a surge of elation. All at once he was wide-awake and bursting with energy. He had been right all along. Pick up the chips and walk away, he thought. Run away. Up to that moment the money had been more fantasy than reality. It had been pieces of paper: deeds to property he had never seen, stock certificates, numbers in a passbook. Suddenly he could feel the texture of real money. The thought brought an itching sensation to his palms and he almost broke out laughing. All those cash payments and bonuses and inside information began to ring up like a supermarket cash register inside his head. How much? he wondered. Millions.

"So I've finally got you to see the light, Amos," he said boastfully. "What did I say that reached you?"

"Nothing. You can be sure I don't share your glee, or your greed. It will take me years to rebuild a cryonic facility of this level of sophistication. I'm sure you don't give a damn about that, but here is something that might interest even you."

Stepp lifted a thick manila folder from his desk. Victor's jaw dropped. He instantly knew where he had seen it before.

"That's Bundy's file on Nancy, Amos. Where did you get it?" Victor asked without wanting to know the answer.

Stepp carried it in on both hands across the office to his discreetly wood-covered paper shredder. "I wanted you to see it first, John. Just so you would never be tempted by some fit of remorse over your wife's fate to unburden yourself. Of course, that is not why I killed him."

"What had he found out, Amos?"

"Nothing, really." Stepp shrugged. "But he would have, in due course. Bundy was quite a good doctor, you know. Actually, you wouldn't. Look at the size of this thing. He had all the information he needed. It was just a matter of synthesizing it. And that would be just a matter of time. A piece here and there and it would all have fallen into place. Most important, John, unlike you, Bundy would never have given up. He showed me this file. That was his mistake. To discredit me would have meant discrediting cryonic research. I could not permit that to happen."

The shredder's blades hummed as Stepp fed it the folder. Victor watched Bundy's notes turn to confetti. "You crazy bastard," he whispered under his breath. "So what if he found anything, Amos? Who gives a damn? You said yourself we'd be long gone."

"You'll never understand, John," Stepp answered scornfully. "God knows, I respect Bundy vastly more than a vain fool like you. Nancy too. She served cryonic research. One day you'll have to tell me just what it was you poured in her drink that ever induced her to consider wasting the rest of her life with the likes of you, John."

"Respect, my ass. You needed both of us, so you used both of us. Only, Nancy got the shitty end of the stick. Amos, there is nothing you could say that would bother me now. If you want to take all this phony bullshit seriously, that's your problem. Play the mad scientist with your own money. High ideals certainly didn't stop you from hogging every dime you could get, and killing anyone who got in your way. Now you've called those press jerks in here, so let's go see them and go out with a bang like a couple of first-class con men. Then, tonight, we can be sipping martinis on the Concorde while NAC goes out with a bang."

23

The lighting rapidly grew better. They climbed a short flight of stairs and the cinder blocks gave way to tiled floors and freshly painted walls. Addison followed closely behind Willie, unconsciously adopting his quick, light-footed stride. He assumed they were, at the very least, unwelcome. The minor offense he might give NAC was not nearly as troubling to him as having only the vaguest notion of what it was Willie meant to accomplish. He was not used to sneaking into buildings. But just what rights did he have? he wondered. Certainly not the right to overrule Nancy's husband and doctor. He remembered the tank, standing in the center of a room like a gleaming torpedo wired up to a life-support system. He saw Nancy's face, ash white through a haze of frozen nitrogen. If that happened again, then Addison could think of no way short of the barrel of a gun to get her out. He wanted to grab Willie by his bony shoulders and shake him until some straight answers came rattling from his mouth. Instead, he continued to follow along. As frustrating as he found Willie's behavior, he knew that without him he would be aimlessly pacing the floor of his hotel room. Anything, he thought, even Willie Garvin, was better than that.

Doors closed behind them as the corridor branched out toward the vast center of the building. Willie guided them through the labyrinth with confident familiarity. At the bottom of a flight of stairs, which Addison assumed was the basement level, he drew to an abrupt halt.

"This is as far as we can go looking like civilians," he announced, while thumbing through the heavy brass key ring he had taken from his pocket. When he located the one he wanted, he slipped it into the lock of a plain green door.

"Hey, anybody in here?" he shouted. When no response came back, he winked at Addison. "Never hurts to check, Bill. The boys might be playing in the shower."

They had walked into a large locker room. Stacks of starched white uniforms were laid out on benches beside each row of footlockers. Willie scampered over to the laundry bins against the far wall.

"Just dump your old stuff in here and NAC will have it back to you tomorrow morning, cleaned and pressed. For you, Mr. A., I'd suggest something in a conservatively cut bedpan emptier's frock. Size forty-four should do nicely."

"Well done, Willie," Addison responded. "Now we can sneak around in style." He glanced at the clock on the wall. It read eight-twenty. "How much time have we got?"

"Just enough to get cleaned up. NAC does not employ scruffies."

Addison was surprised. A shower and shave had taken ten years off his guess at Willie's age. His gray hair had become shiny and black. Addison could not determine which look had been the disguise.

Willie noticed his stare and leered back at him. "NAC does not employ any old fags, either, Bill. So now that we both look like part of the staff, I'll lead you to Nancy."

There was an unfamiliar whine in Willie's voice and for a moment Addison thought he heard a twinge of jealousy. He decided to ignore it.

"Willie, you've done very well so far," he said. "But can you really tell me that you know where, in this four acre building, they've put Nancy? Willie, just what the hell did you do here?"

The brightness slipped from Willie's eyes and his cheeks turned beet red. "I was her keeper, Bill."

Addison leaned forward as though his ears might have played some trick on him. Willie stood hangdog-still for a moment, like an embarrassed child. Then he burst past Addison, out of the locker room. Addison lunged, but the smaller man eluded his grasp. He dived after him, bursting into the corridor like a drunk reeling out of a saloon. Only the sight of other people yanked him back to the pretense of normal posture. When he saw Willie turn at the end of the corridor, he wanted to bolt after him. All the statistics Bendel had given him sank down to the memory of one live rat curled in a glass cage. Only the creatures that started out alive could be thawed out. Bundy made the same connection. Willie did know who had killed him. Now Addison was sure that he knew too. NAC.

Willie paused at a stairwell just long enough for Addison to pick him out from the other white-jacketed men who had begun to fill the corridor. His eyes had regained their sparkle and he flashed a wide grin. His thumb flicked upward. Addison slowed his pace to match those around him. There was no longer any need to run. He knew Willie was reeling him in like a fish on a line.

As he expected, Willie was waiting at the top of the next landing. He put a finger to his lips and pointed at the sign above the red exit light.

CRYONIC STORAGE AREA
AUTHORIZED PERSONNEL ONLY

The notion of a warehouse full of packing crates flashed through Addison's brain.

"They're frauds, aren't they, Willie? You were some part of it, and now they're after you. They can't bring any of those people back. They just took their money and stuffed their bodies into some fancy-looking tanks. They were dead before they were frozen, and dead they will stay. Nancy survived because she was still alive when they put her into cryonic suspension. But nobody made the connection, except maybe Bundy."

"Not too shabby, Bill." Willie nodded approvingly. "Now I can see why you get the big money. Nice-looking, sharp mind, waspy nose . . . Go prove it. You think Amos Stepp is a jerk. So you get yourself a court order or something, and have the stiffs melted out. All you'll have is a lot of smelly bad meat and a big raspberry from Dr. Stepp. He would laugh his ass off. You'd take him right off the hook. For the public he'd be all teary and full of righteous indignation. He wasn't given a fair chance. Remember, he started with dead bodies. You can't do much to hurt a dead body."

"What about Nancy? She was certified dead. But that's impossible, isn't it? Listen to me, dammit," he hissed. "What the hell did you mean back there. What is a 'keeper'?"

Willie ignored the question. He took a plastic identification card from his pocket and slipped it into a computer reader mounted on the door lock.

"No doubt about it, Bill. Nancy is the great success story that made it all possible," he finally answered in the offhand tone of one who has barely heard the question. Most of his attention was centered on punching a digital code number into the palm-sized keyboard set in the door just above the card reader. His index finger was poised for the final number, but he paused. His brow wrinkled and his lips curled into a sheepish smile.

"You'd better hold on to your hat, Bill," he said. The instant he hit the key, a shrill siren exploded through the narrow stairwell. Addison held his ears. He could feel the vibration of footsteps pounding up to the door.

"What the hell did you do?" he screamed at Willie. In his brain he could see a cage slamming shut. There was absolutely no place to run.

Willie snapped his fingers with displeasure. "I guess I hit the wrong button," he replied.

The door swung open and the siren cut off. Only the ringing in Addison's ears continued. He looked up at the two men who stared out of the light at them.

"Phil," Willie said warmly. "I betcha I scared the shit out of you guys."

The shorter, stout man immediately extended a hairy hand. "You schmuck, Willie," he said with feigned irritation. "Don't you know we can get into trouble for opening this door? Come on, get the hell in here before Security pick you up and kick your ass around the block. Frank . . ." he shouted back over his shoulder. "Call Security. Tell them we had a short in the wires. Otherwise them bastards will come running in here with their guns waving."

"Yeah," the man at the console answered. "What's new in fagdom, Willie? We figured you'd be around someplace, what with Nancy back for a return engagement."

Addison focused his attention on the laboratory behind the control room's glass wall. It was the size of a small auditorium, with chairs set up like a lecture hall, and so brightly lit that the tile and chrome fixtures sparkled like mica in the sun. People in business suits were filling the seats that tiered upward, movie-house-style. Others milled around the television cameras set up at the front of the room. These spectators set themselves well apart from the crew of workmen busily engaged in rearranging laboratory gear. Tables were being wheeled out a wide double door at the far end, while portable computer display equipment was rolling in, like heavy traffic through a tunnel.

"What's going on, Phil?" Addison asked in his best one-of-the-boys tone.

"Who the hell did you bring with you?" The skinny man at the console turned his anger on Willie. "You know damned well that you can get into a shitload of trouble by sneaking around."

"Don't mind Frankie, Bill. He's always been a nerd. For your information, Bill just started working for me. I'm giving him the fifty-cent tour," he announced. "If you want to make a big deal out of my punching the wrong ID number, go ahead. I dare you."

Frankie sank back in his seat. The third man, who had remained silent, offered his hand to Addison. He had a broad, friendly face and appeared to want no part of the others' bickering.

"Name's Arty, Bill. We monitor the environment in the lab. It's not such a big deal 'tween times, like now. Just a matter of keeping the reporters comfortable and the lights bright enough for the cameras. But when the doctors are doing a body-wash operation, we've got to stay on top of the temperature, humidity, bacteria filtration, oxygen, CO_2, gas exchange, hell of a lot more. That operating room has to be one-hundred-percent sterile. Some poor dead bastard's got his guts spread all over the table, we got to make sure it's clean."

"What's going on out there now?" Addison asked.

Arty shrugged. "The boss called some kind of press conference. He likes to use the operating room. Thinks it's classy or something. Jesus, he used to do it all the time. Things have quieted down the last couple of weeks." Then he turned to Willie. "I heard you were fired. You and that big dumb guy who'd hang around with you. Kovachek or—"

"I took some personal time," Willie answered sharply. Only Addison noticed the flash of fear that brightened his eyes for an instant before he spoke. The others accepted the answer and returned to their consoles.

It dawned on Addison that a hundred people on the other side of the glass could have been watching, just as he could look out on them. But a workman's uniform proved effective camouflage. Nobody paid any attention. They had begun to settle into their seats. A youngish, well-dressed man waited patiently behind a dais that had been wheeled in only moments before. Willie leaned over Frank's shoulder and flipped a switch on his console. The auditorium speaker system crackled through the small control room.

"Ladies and gentlemen," the young man began. "Dr. Stepp will be with us in just a few more minutes. He has already left his office—"

There was a flurry of activity in the auditorium. Heads turned like they were on swivels. Stepp emerged from the rear door. He waved to the seated reporters like a beauty queen on her way down the aisle to accept her trophy. John Victor led a tight cadre of executives who followed a respectful distance behind. They filled the front row of seats while Stepp made himself comfortable behind the freshly vacated dais.

Addison glanced over his shoulder. He saw that Willie had shrunk back against the far wall. But the control room was a fishbowl with no dark corners. He watched the little man wriggle like a worm on a hook. Finally he found a spot of relative safety, crouching behind Phil's wide shoulders.

Frankie leered with satisfaction. "What's the matter, Willie?" he minced. "You paint a mustache on Nancy's pretty face and now you're afraid the boss will kick your ass when the press boys see her?"

Willie almost jumped. "Nancy?" he blurted out.

The others stared at him for a moment.

"What the hell did you think was going on?" Frankie asked sarcastically. "Shit, even we're smart enough to figure that one out."

Then Addison saw the tank, and he, too, knew why the press had come. Heads swung from Stepp to the double doors. It emerged slowly, balanced on the tines of a forklift, just above the ground. For a moment it looked like a bullet on end, gliding across a frozen pond. Its array of tubes and wires was reeled out from the laboratory behind the doors. The computer displays suddenly lit up with bright green blips on their dark screens. The forklift stopped beside the dais. Nancy was looking right at him. From fifty feet away he could see her face through the wispy mist behind the plastic front plate. He pressed his nose against the window and strained his eyes for a better look. It was Nancy, exactly as she had been the last time, when he was forced to view her from behind a velvet rope. As though the tank had captured her and returned her to the same point in time. Exactly. Addison looked again. The memory had become part of him, and with it his sadness returned.

Stepp was speaking. ". . . and by the time we reached Miss Seymour, it was clear that her military fever had become life-threatening. I must admit that what we, at NAC, had believed was a cure had only succeeded in bringing her condition into a state of remission. We had no choice but to immediately place her into a state of cryonic suspension. That was the only certain life-saving step—"

Hands shot up all over the auditorium. Several reporters were already on their feet. The questions Addison heard came from a dozen mouths at once.

"Do you mean she was alive when you froze her?" someone shouted out. "Dr. Stepp, the law is clear on this point. Cryonic suspension is only valid after a certificate of death has been issued. Has NAC knowingly broken the law?"

Stepp stretched his hands out across the dais. His eyes were cast downward like a mendicant pleading for alms. Addison could see John Victor's profile as he leaned forward. His skin was almost as white as Nancy's.

"Miss Seymour's husband—my associate and friend Dr. Victor—and I were forced to make that decision," he continued in a voice barely above a whisper. Addison thought Victor might pitch forward right out of his chair. "We had to weigh the law against the consequences of inaction. We made our decision and will stand accountable for it."

Bendel's rat. She can survive, Addison thought with a rush of relief.

"Bullshit!" Willie Garvin's shout shattered the control room's quiet hum of efficiency. Addison spun around as Willie wrenched open the door to the auditorium. "Stepp, you lie!" he shouted again. For a moment the large room was dead silent with shock. Addison anticipated Willie's next move and started for the doorway. He was too late. Willie charged across the front of the auditorium like an actor leaping in from the wings. He darted along the narrow aisle that separated the dais from the first row of seats.

Addison bolted after him, realizing what would happen the moment he tried to attack Stepp. In one quick glance he picked out the security guards from the journalists. Even in unobtrusive plain clothes, they were clearly younger and far stronger. But to Addison's eye the surest test was that they were already on their feet, moving for their weapons.

"Don't shoot!" his voice boomed over the confusion of noises. "He's unarmed."

To his surprise, Willie dodged the dais, completely ignoring Stepp. Addison was only a few yards behind, leading the surge of technicians that had joined the pursuit. Then, in a flash, he knew Willie's goal. Stepp knew too. Addison was directly in front of the dais when the microphone barked in his ears.

"Stop that murderer!" Stepp screamed in a frenzy, pounding his fists on the dais.

Willie lunged at the tank. He embraced it with both arms like a cat wrapping its paws around a thick tree. The tank quivered on its forklift perch, but Willie's weight was insufficient to tip it. His right hand clutched the wrist-thick liquid-nitrogen tube at the very top. The audience shrank back. Even the security men froze in their tracks. Willie burst into a high-pitched laugh. Addison saw madness in his flashing blue eyes. The tank was his hostage. If he wrenched the hose loose, or even punctured it ever so slightly, the flow of liquid nitrogen exposed to room temperature would ignite like a bathtub full of napalm. Willie puffed himself up, basking in the fear that hung over the auditorium. His laugh grew louder, like a symphony building to a crescendo.

"Shoot him!" Stepp ordered the guards, flailing both arms in the air like a child throwing a tantrum. It was the last sound Addision expected to hear. He picked out half a dozen men with handguns poised.

Suddenly Willie switched his grip from the hose to a ganglion of color-coded electrical wires. He leaped off the tank, yanking a handful of the wires from their soldered connections. The tank shot out a fountain of sparks that arced like a welder's torch. The flash was bright as a phosphorous flare. Acrid blue ozone smoke belched from the torn connection. Addison shot an arm up to cover his eyes and mouth just as the lights flickered and went out. He groped blindly toward the tank. His mind raced in a dozen directions at once as the smoke seared his lungs. He pounded on the front plate. Willie murdered her, he thought. He robbed her of her last slim chance. She'll thaw in minutes. She has no immunities. Any bacteria could kill her. He had to get her out of the tank. His hands groped for the clasp that would pop the plate free. Then he would hold her in his arms and breathe the life back into her body. He felt other hands on the tank and wrenched them aside. The confusion of noises and pounding feet belonged to another world. He barely heard the voice shouting just over his shoulder.

"Be calm. Everyone keep their seats!" Stepp yelled into a dead microphone. "The power will be restored in just a moment. Nobody is to touch the tank."

The smoke grew thicker. It burned Addison's eyes like an acid mist. Fire sirens went off in his head. A hand caught his wrist and tugged him back. Even in the pitch-blackness he knew it was Willie. He twisted the fingers around until he heard a sharp squeal of pain.

"You killed her, you son of a bitch," he shouted into the darkness.

"Bill, we've got to get out of here," Willie urged.

Addison did not believe his ears. "You got me to help you do this." He twisted harder, listening for the snap of bone.

"Let go, you fool. That's not Nancy in there," Willie burst

out in pain and anger. "We've only got a minute until the lights come back on. Bill, you know what will happen if they catch us. You've got to trust me."

Willie's voice was persuasive beyond logic; it rang with the timbre of honesty that would bring an Eskimo out in the cold to buy a block of ice.

"Nancy's not dead?" Addison repeated as though Willie's answer would make it true. Willie tugged him again, and this time he followed. Suddenly it came to him, like a burst of clarity in the darkness, just why it was he trusted Willie Garvin. It was the look in his eyes every time he mentioned Nancy's name. Addison knew where he had seen that look before. In his shaving mirror, every morning. He loved her too.

Willie moved like a bat through a cave, slowing down only to make sure that Addison was keeping pace. They pushed through the swinging doors into the laboratory. The red emergency lights cast long, dim shadows through the billowing smoke. Addison picked out the shapes moving toward the center of the room. Their activity was dim as a television screen through a shower curtain. They groped along the outlines of their equipment. The shouts between them could have come from survivors clinging to debris in a choppy sea. Addison felt the wall brushing his back as Willie led him around the periphery of the large room. Then he felt a door open behind him. The auxiliary lighting in the hallway was almost bright by comparison.

"We're almost out," Willie whispered. "Just be cool a little longer."

The lights came back with a rush of energy that started the air-conditioning motors clattering. Addison saw little of the urgency he had expected in the faces of the people he passed. They were buzzing, as anyone would, after a power failure. But nothing more. Willie ignored his surprise, ushering him toward the exit light that seemed a mile away down the long, bare hallway.

"Why the hell hasn't Stepp put out a general alarm?" he asked Willie. "He knew you. He should have had us nailed before we got out of the laboratory."

"Maybe Amos doesn't forget his friends. Oh, we're not out of these woods yet. But no cops, Billy. Stepp wouldn't dare do that. Just keep an eye out for his personal goon squad. They're the nasty-looking dudes in the crisp blue uniforms."

Addison shot a glance back over his shoulder. The working people they passed looked tame enough to open a bank.

"What about Nancy? I saw her in that damned tank when you pulled the plug."

"So it would appear," Willie answered with a wry smile. They were almost at the exit when he tucked his arm under Addison's and guided him through a narrow unmarked doorway. Three more doors ringed a small square foyer.

"This will only take a minute, Billy. I thought you'd like to see where I used to work."

Willie already had the key in his hand. Addison sensed the futility of arguing haste. He knew he was being led like a bull with a ring in his nose. Willie turned the key and shoved open the door.

"Voilà!" he announced with a wave of his hand. The room was neither office nor laboratory. It was large and very brightly lit, and for a moment Addison was at a loss to describe its function. The walls were lined with bulbed stage mirrors and racks of colorful clothes. Willie pushed a button beside the light switch, and disco music began to blare from unseen speakers.

"A boutique?" Addison asked.

"A magic shop," Willie corrected. "Every chemical company that gets itself into the cryonics business should have at least one. Now I show you the Nancy Seymour you think I killed."

His fingers traced the outline of a panel set into the wall. At the right pressure point it popped open, exposing a cipher box. He punched in six digits. The mirrored wall spun like a revolving door. Addison felt a flash of cold fear, then pure surprise. He took a closer look. For an instant he would have sworn that Nancy had been staring at him from a half-dozen cubicles mounted on the reverse side of the swinging wall. Her heads were displayed like an executioner's trophy case. Each one captured a mood that ran from joy to sadness. Each one was perfect. Addison's fingers were drawn to stroke the texture of her skin. Even under the bright lights he found the small lines around her mouth and eyes, all as perfect as a studio photograph.

"My work," Willie shouted jubilantly. "All my work, every one of them. See how her lips pout when she is angry. And the slightest flaring of her nostrils. That one up there." He directed Addison's gaze. "That one is my special favorite. What you saw in the tank was mine too. Not that I like it very much. Too dour. That's not my Nancy. We know her better. But it even fooled you, Billy. Stepp only wanted that one. The Death Face, he called it. That cheap, tacky shit. All that money he's ripping off, and he had no use for my art.

"Billy, do you know that he actually ordered me to destroy these. He thinks they're all gone." Willie's tone had turned into an irritating whine. But Addison grasped his message and rushed to cut him off.

"If Nancy wasn't in the tank, where have they got her? And why the hell did you bother pulling that stupid stunt?"

Willie's look turned quizzical. "Don't you think I owed Stepp a kick in the ass? Let's see him weasel out of that little fracas. Besides, how else would I have gotten you to see my art? I couldn't have taken you directly here. You'd have been rush, rush, rush, where-is-Nancying me to death. You had to be fooled a little bit, Billy. Now you can tell Nancy how perfect they really are. She's never seen them, you see. And even if she does, it won't be the same. But you'll tell her that you were fooled. You'll admit it, won't you Billy?"

Addison could see that he was talking to a time bomb. Willie's neck veins had begun to bulge. His pupils were widely dilated and his breath came in short fast gasps. Addison had to hold him together a little longer.

"Willie, I'll arrange your own exclusive one-man show on Madison Avenue," he said carefully, watching for some reaction. Willie broke into a narrow smile. His breath slowed. "Your work is remarkable. I'm going to tell that to Nancy the minute I see her. Now, you've got to take me to her, and we've got to get the hell out of this building."

"Oh, stop fretting, Billy. You'll get worry lines," Willie chided. His mood had swung to serenity. "Uncle Amos isn't going to let any policeman open his tank to find a waxy victim."

"Where is she, Willie?" Addison pressed.

"Not so far away, I think. We can go save her now, Billy. Now that you've seen my Nancys, it's important that you compare them with the real thing. I like the idea of Amos sweating it out with those reporters, and all the while he's really worried sick over what we're doing. Don't think he doesn't know what we're after. I'll teach that bald creep a lesson. He can't push Willie Garvin around."

"Willie, he hasn't even started pushing you. You've gotten Dr. Stepp very angry."

The voice froze them for an instant. Then Addison spun around. Two uniformed men stood blocking the open doorway. Their guns were drawn.

"Holy shit. Will you look at those fucking heads," the second one exclaimed.

Willie jumped between his work and their amazed stares like a mother hen protecting her flock. He slapped the encoder panel and the wall spun back to a blank mirror. "Mind your own business," he snapped at them. "Now, come on, Billy, we're leaving. These goons won't dare bother us."

Addison did not see it that way. The hard-eyed men in the doorway were just the sort he would have hired for a nasty piece of work. Loose-fitting suits hardly concealed their lean, athletic bodies.

"Come along peacefully," one of them responded, unmoved by Willie's taunt. "You too, Mr. Addison. We haven't got all day."

Willie held his ground, hands defiantly planted on his hips. Compared to the tough security men, he looked no more menacing than a small, ill-mannered child.

The one who had spoken shrugged his shoulders. "You want to make it tough on yourself, asshole, that's going to be your problem."

He advanced to grab Willie's arm. His movement was quick and sure. Willie sprang backward. A silver tube flashed in his hand. Addison covered his eyes just as a spray of fine mist burst from its tip. The guard recoiled, gasping desperately for air. His eyes rolled back into his head and his knees buckled under him. Addison spun toward the second man. The pistol in his hand cut through the air like a club aimed at Addison's head. Addison flicked out his forearm to deflect the blow and his open right hand shot forward. He chopped the guard flush across the throat. The force of the blow sent him reeling backward, his feet flying out from under him. He shattered a mirrored wall into a spray of glass slivers and sank slowly to the floor. Willie was already halfway out the door. Addison felt a rush of energy such as he had not felt in months. Both doors slammed and locked behind them.

They paused a moment at the edge of the parking lot. A siren wailed somewhere on the far side of the building.

"Don't be so cheerful, Billy," Willie said as he opened the door of his car. "Dr. Stepp has a pretty fancy notion of where to catch up with us."

At Stepp's signal the guards had formed a tight cordon around the tank. Almost immediately the crew from the laboratory began backing it through the door and out of sight. Stepp held his ground on the dais, glaring out at his audience like a lion tamer in front of a hungry pride. They were on their feet, some gathering their senses, but mostly shouting questions. For a moment he wished he could summon back the darkness and ozone smoke. He was almost afraid to look squarely at the tank for fear Nancy's face had melted into a gob of soft wax.

"No. I cannot assure you that no damage was done. I must begin tests immediately," he shouted frantically. "I assure you that you will be kept completely informed. Everyone at NAC sincerely regrets the unpleasant incident you were forced to witness. I'm afraid that is all I have time to say."

He had no intention of answering the barrage of questions concerning the exact nature of the tests he had in mind. But one question caught his ear and he turned back to the microphone.

"Yes, I did recognize the . . . vandal. A former employee named Willie Garvin."

Everybody scribbled.

"I'm confident that the police will have no difficulty apprehending him," he concluded. The guards who had been protecting the tank moved quickly to his side. The print reporters were already streaming out the rear exits. He caught sight of the public-relations man who had first warmed up his audience. He was pale enough to have spent a month in the tank himself.

Stepp took a firm hold on his elbow and pulled him close. "The police will be here any second, George," he whispered.

"Give them everything they want on Willie. Everything but me. Tell them I'm in Surgery. I trust you will do a better job than my security people have managed so far."

George nodded solemnly. He was very glad that he had nothing whatever to do with security.

Victor maneuvered through a mob of technicians and security guards. He stopped in his tracks the moment he got a clear view of the tank. A smile spread across his face. His pounding heart slowed. He moved in for a closer examination. Every step buoyed his confidence. The mask was perfectly intact. Who else knows, who else shares my relief? he wondered. He glanced around quickly for anyone blowing out a sigh as heartfelt as his own. Everybody wore a professional poker face, like a moon launch had just been aborted but was all in a day's work. You can't tell the Ins from the Outs without a scorecard, he thought. That clever bastard Stepp plays it close to the vest. Four or five millionaires who do all the real work and a bunch of stiffs in white coats pushing meaningless buttons. It is always handy to leave a few flunkies behind to take the heat while we're living it up in Brazil. He was counting the hours to takeoff. Willie and Addison can't hurt you now, he thought. You're too close. Willie's got no trump card. He can't go to the cops. If Addison knew what Willie really did, he'd kill him. Victor smirked. Willie hasn't spilled his guts in the last six months, and he is not about to do it now. He knows damned well that he'd fry right along with us.

Still, Victor would have been a good deal more comfortable if he were certain that Security had stopped them before they got off the grounds. But nothing at all seemed to be troubling Dr. Stepp. Victor heard him barking out orders like a general directing his troops. Showman to the last, he decided. He idly watched while the electricians replaced the burned-out circuit panel in the nose of the tank.

"John, over here," Stepp called out. He was beaming and radiant. He slapped Victor on the shoulder and led him to a far corner of the laboratory. "Well, that little weasel Garvin finally did us a favor," he said, enjoying Victor's confusion. "God, you are thick. Don't you see it, John? Get to a safe phone. Call the farm. Tell Melnick to prepare Nancy's body for autopsy and get her back here immediately. Then find out where Security is holding Garvin and Addison. I want them separated. That way Garvin can have a little accident. Then he can posthumously take the fall for Bundy's murder too. You see, John, all things unfold as they should."

24

Willie screeched to a halt on the shoulder of the narrow two-lane road. He shot a finger at a driveway fifty yards away. It was a barely visible strip of asphalt bordered by a crumbling stone wall. Nothing was visible beyond the road save trees and dense overgrown shrubbery. But once off the main roads, all the back-country property was kept in a natural state. This piece was indistinguishable from anything else they had passed on the ten-minute breakneck drive. Addison recalled an old adage: you can get anyplace in a car in ten minutes if you drive fast enough.

"That's where they've got her, Billy. I'm sure of it," Willie said. He was panting like an overweight jogger. Beads of sweat glistened on his forehead. "Now we can only pray that she is still alive."

"What the hell is this place? Is it part of NAC?"

"Follow me," Willie ordered, ignoring Addison's questions. He opened the trunk of the car and handed Addison a toolbox. Then he took out a thin, tightly rolled mattress tied up with string. Addison followed him across the road and up a small incline to the base of the wall. He crouched down and quickly untied his mattress.

"Billy, the problem with being a crook, even a smart crook

like Stepp, is that you can't trust anybody. But there's just no way around it. Like he had to trust me. This was his special place. The farm." Willie spat out the words, his lips curling in disgust. "He installed lots of high-priced electronic gear but it's staffed with as few people as possible. Just be very careful and follow my footsteps. I know where all the land mines are laid."

Addison gingerly ran his fingers along the top of the seven-foot-high wall. As he had expected the moment Willie produced the mattress, the top was laced with jagged shards of broken glass embedded in a layer of concrete.

"Right on," Willie said. "The Glastonbury zoning board doesn't exactly appreciate tacky triple-strand barbed wire and machine-gun towers. Looks bad on the real-estate ads. Stepp had to be a little cooler, at least on the outside of the place."

Willie tossed the mattress over the wall and tugged on the end. The glass gripped it fast, like a gaff in a fish's belly. He wiped the sweat off his palms and managed a weak smile. "Wait until you see the improvements that he didn't bother to mention. You ready?"

Addison locked his fingers together for a foothold. Willie tested his grip.

"Go," he said.

Addison lifted sharply and Willie sprang for the top of the wall. He let out a squeal of pain as he rolled over and out of sight. A long stain of blood spread down the mattress.

"I'm okay. I'm okay," Willie wimpered from the other side. "Be careful. The fuckin' glass cut right through."

Addison wished he could think of a safer way. He tossed the toolbox over. Then he carefully found a handhold on the top of the mattress and pulled himself up. He could see the glass, sharp as razor blades, sticking through in half a dozen places. He swung a leg up beside his hand and jumped clear. His feet hit the ground inches from Willie's head. The small man sat crumpled up like a ball, bony knees tucked under his chin. His white lab coat was smeared with blood.

"I'll be all right. It looks worse than it is," he said evenly. But Addison saw tears of pain rolling down his cheeks. He unclenched Willie's fist and examined the deep gash across his palm. Then he felt the dampness on the back of his hand. The glass had ripped clear through.

"You stay here," Addison insisted. He looked around at

the wall of shrubbery that hemmed in the small clearing. "Which way is it?"

Willie shook his head vehemently. "Help me up," he gasped. "You'll never make it alone. It'll take both of us to save Nancy. I spent eight months in this rotten place. I know every inch of it. You need me."

Addison sensed he was right. There was no time for trial and error or for noble gestures. He took Willie under the arms and lifted him to his feet. He was still bleeding.

"We can do it. We can do it, Billy," Willie chanted. The words seemed to give him strength. "I can walk, and I know a way that even Stepp never found. But first things first. We've got a little trick to play on the bastards."

Addison gingerly parted a clump of thorny bushes. He held them so Willie could squirm through. Suddenly they burst into the sunlight like divers coming up for air. They had emerged at the edge of a long, rolling lawn. Addison stared up at the old stone house. It was three stories high, turreted at all four corners, and big enough to be called a mansion. The driveway, bordered by weathered oak trees, bisected the lawn. As it approached the house it forked off to a garage and an outbuilding that was originally used as a stable. There was a twenty-foot antenna mounted on its roof. An ambulance was parked in front of the house.

"She's still here," Willie exclaimed. "They weren't taking any chances. They wanted her well out of sight during the press conference." •

"How many people does Stepp have on the property, Willie?"

"Five or six. But only two would ever see Nancy. The others don't know what's going on. They just guard the place and mow the lawns. Look, that's where we've got to go." He pointed at a shed, separated from the main house by a large cluster of trees.

Addison judged it to be at least a hundred yards away, most of it across wide-open lawn. He studied Willie's face. His skin was as pallid as Nancy's death mask. "You'll never make it," he said. "You could barely walk that far."

"Not if the goons were on their toes and looking for me. Open the toolbox, Billy. We're going to zap them good. They'll be so fucked up that we could waltz in there."

It took Addison a moment to recognize the black cylinder.

He had seen versions of it in the cockpit of F-16 fighters, but never in a battered tin box.

"How the hell did you get your hands on a Rocky?" he asked with surprise, and no little admiration. The football-sized communications-distortion module tapered to a broad-tipped LED snout, giving it the general appearance of a raccoon when seen from the front. Even the cheaper, export models were highly restricted and sold only to friendly powers. Addison had seen it raise hell with ground-to-air communications.

"Rocky—is that what it's called? Very cute. I bought it," Willie said proudly. "With my NAC stock-option money. Stepp cheated me out of most of my money, but even I made a few bucks—off poor Nancy. The guy who sold it to me worked for our military electronics division. We had a thing—" he began wistfully.

"Knock it off," Addison cut in.

"Well, I was smart enough to get it. You weren't. I knew I'd be coming back here one day. I've been carting it around for months. I always meant to read the instruction book, but . . . God, I hope you know how it works."

"Microwave oscillation."

"No. I mean can you make the fucking thing work? I can't even understand the dials."

The handle had been fastened to the top of the instrument almost as an afterthought. Addison pointed its nose at the ground like a Geiger counter. The controls were awkwardly set in a rear panel, reflecting its primary function as an aircraft-console-mounted insert.

Willie nodded in the direction of the antenna. "Stepp put in his own little power station. Even a small cryonics lab like the one he's got here draws a hell of a lot more juice than all the surveillance gear put together. I guess Stepp figured it would raise a few eyebrows at the local utility if a nice quiet gent was running a ten-thou-a-month electric tab. So he operates like Dr. Frankenstein and keeps the townies in the dark."

Addison picked out a line of sight and activated the CDM. Its nose light began to glow, but it made no sound or gave any other evidence of functioning. The antenna remained motionless, reflecting morning sunshine off its polished-metal surfaces.

"Is it working?" Willie asked quickly.

Addison set it on the ground, just at the edge of the bushes. "If their next telephone call sounds like Donald Duck speaking pig latin, it's working." Addison could make out the distant shapes of two men moving between the garage and the main house. "But we're going to have to trip a detector to find out."

Victor traded his pin-striped suit coat for a white technician's jacket. Then he took the long route back to his office. Even with these precautions, he was surprised that absolutely nobody appeared to recognize him. He knew perfectly well that Stepp could not have gone ten feet in a gorilla costume without being acknowledged. The very success of his ploy aroused a twinge of jealousy. He was even more jealous of Stepp's nimble brain. Produce Nancy's body, traumatically jerked from cryonic suspension. He could frame his own headlines: "NANCY SEYMOUR MURDERED WHEN POWER GOES OUT." All those millions of people saw Willie do it. He pictured the freeze frames and close-ups and slow-motion shots that would dominate the news. Then Willie gets himself snuffed in the course of our legitimate restraint. Case closed. He only wished there was some way to implicate Addison too.

He kept the direct-line phone in a locked drawer of his desk. Its only purpose was to contact the farm. Since very few people at NAC knew of the existence of the farm, it was not the sort of thing to be left lying carelessly exposed.

He lifted the receiver to his ear, knowing there would be an immediate acknowledgment. It came as squawking gibberish over the din of a rusty typewriter banging out ninety words per minute.

Fear froze Victor to the floor. His face became flushed. He could feel his pulse racing. He tossed the receiver on his desk as though he had been holding a hot poker.

"Get me Security!" he shouted into the intercom.

"Forget it," Stepp yelled from across the room. For a moment the small, squat man looked ten feet tall. "They got away. Both of them."

Suddenly Victor realized that he had made a terrible mistake. "I can't get through to the farm. Something is wrong with the communications," he stuttered. He would have said more, but he thought Stepp might kill him on the spot.

"Get them on the shortwave band, you idiot. If Addison finds Nancy's body at the farm . . ."

Victor shook his head from side to side. It was all the mobility his fear would permit. "There is no body, Amos. I . . . used your name. I told them not to kill her. She's my wife, Amos."

"We'll settle this matter of insubordination later, John. Right now you're going to do as you're told. Then we're going up to the farm to make sure it's finished for good and all."

A fat well digger's got no future at all, Addison thought. He had to lean forward over the thick cluster of water pipes and slip sideways across the slimy floor of the access tunnel. It was uphill. He dragged his body from handhold to handhold, stepping gingerly so his feet would not fly out from under him. Willie's smaller size fit far more comfortably into the confines of the tunnel. But his wound had drained his strength. His hand slipped from the rung. Addison heard it and looked back at him.

"Billy, it would be a hell of a lot easier if we were coming down from the house," he said. "I've got to rest a minute."

Even the dim safety lights were bright enough for Addison to see that his hand had begun to swell. Dark pinheads of blood appeared under his fingernails.

"How much farther is it, Willie?" he asked. Looking up the tunnel, all he could see was the glow of unevenly spaced light bulbs that distorted his judgment of distance. The aches in his body told him that they had already covered more than enough ground.

"I'm not sure. I think we're under the house now. I only did it once. It can't be much farther. God, it stinks in here."

"Hang on to my belt. I'll pull you the rest of the way."

The tunnel widened slightly and began to level off. The ground under their feet was almost dry. Addison's stare followed the pipes. They ran into the back of a water tank the size of an oil truck. He forgot about the weight he was hauling and quickened his pace. His eyes remained riveted straight ahead, but in the back of his brain he strained for some message that Nancy was near.

Then the tunnel ended in a small dank room that housed the semisubmerged water tank. In the half-light it could have been the carcass of a beached whale. The rest of the room was bare but for a few rusting plumber's tools, rags, and empty beer cans. Addison's eyes lit on a heavy wrench. He hefted it a moment. Only one attendant, Willie had assured him.

"We made it," Willie said in a weak gasp. "The laboratory is just down the hall."

As they reached the door, Willie put a finger to his lips. Then he tucked his bloody hand under his arm and squeezed it hard against his body. "I did wrong, Billy," he said. "I hurt Nancy. Now I'm being punished. Do you think she'll understand?"

"I'll explain it to her, Willie. She'll understand."

Willie shook his head in vague comprehension. "All those months . . ." He sighed. "I took care of her. I never thought I was being cruel."

"You were her keeper," Addison replied. "You were just doing a job. She'll see it that way too. Nancy isn't the sort to carry a grudge."

Willie's face brightened and for a moment Addison could detect the hint of a sparkle returning to his eyes. "Follow me, Billy. And bring your wrench."

He threw the latch and shoved open the rusty iron door. What Addison could see from over his shoulder looked nothing like the basement of an old Connecticut home. It was as though they had emerged back at NAC. Everything was high-gloss and sparkled like a freshly tiled men's room. The doorway was recessed like a side road off the main corridor. Willie motioned Addison to wait out of sight. He pulled himself fully erect and began to whistle loudly. Then he took a jaunty step into the corridor and out of Addison's line of sight. A shout followed almost immediately.

"Garvin? How the hell did you . . . ?"

Addison heard the clatter of footsteps. Willie ran past him in the opposite direction. He pushed himself flush against the alcove wall. The burly man was right on Willie's heels when Addison stepped out behind him. A sharp blow of the wrench cracked open the back of his head. He dropped like a stone in a pool of blood. Willie reached for his feet, but Addison stopped him.

"No time. Leave him here," he said. "We gotta get to Nancy." He tucked the guard's pistol into his belt.

Nancy sensed the footsteps. She could feel the light burning her eyes. The scream stuck in her throat. It was all happening again. The dream. The pain would follow. Then the blood. But always, there was the fear.

"She's dead!" Addison shouted. "We're too late."

Nancy lay on a low pallet covered only by a thin quilt that silhouetted the contours of her body. Addison bolted across the large room. He dropped to his knees beside her. Her lips had shriveled down to thin blue lines. He pressed his hand against her cheek. It was freezing. He brushed her quilt. His hand instinctively recoiled from its numbing cold. He tore it off her body. The hard pallet beneath her was just as cold. He scooped her up and held her like a baby in his arms. She seemed so frail that he sensed she would blow away in a strong wind. Gently he laid her on an operating table and covered her with his jacket.

Willie elbowed in beside him. "No!" he shouted jubilantly. "Thank God. She's not dead. It's hypothermia. Cold soak. Exposure from this miserable place, and God knows what else. Slap her, Billy. Slap her. Keep her awake. I've got to get something to wrap her with."

A moment later Willie came running back with a stack of blankets from the supply closet. Addison pumped her wrists and palms. Then he began to move her head from side to side.

"Come on," he urgently pleaded in her ear. "Don't give up. Not now, Nan."

He pressed an ear to her mouth and held his breath. After a moment he was certain that the thin wisp of warm air he felt had escaped from her lungs.

Then he turned his boiling anger on Willie. "Those bastards were freezing her to death so they could produce the right kind of corpse. That quilt was pumping Freon. She was in an ice pack. Is that what you were a part of?"

Willie jumped backward. "No. Believe me, Bill. I never saw this before. We didn't even keep her here, except once in a while. She had her own room where I took care of her. I bathed her and fed her all those months she thought she was dead. They kept her too drugged up so she wouldn't remember anything. I'd never hurt her, Billy."

"Then why didn't you go to the police? Why did you wait for this to happen?"

"I couldn't. I just couldn't," Willie stammered. Tears welled up in his eyes.

"Angel."

Addison heard Nancy's faint whisper and spun around. Her limp hand was extended, but not to him. Willie fell down beside her and covered it with kisses.

"You saved me again. You save me every time," she said with a flood of gratitude.

Addison thought his ears were playing tricks. But it was Nancy's voice, and her eyes were almost clear as she stared at Willie's face.

"Billy, she remembers," Willie said through his sobs. "She called me an angel then, too."

"When?"

"When I killed for her." His small face contorted into an ugly snarl. "One of the grounds keepers, an animal, tried to . . . violate her. He did. He was on top of her, doing his disgusting thing to my Nancy. He should never have been allowed near her. I caught him. I stabbed him with a scapel. Again and again." He pounded his bloody fist on the edge of the table. "Then Stepp caught me. He said he would help. He'd get rid of the body. But he wouldn't tell me where or how. He just kept on warning me—"

"It's okay, Willie," Addison said gently. He had heard enough. His mind shot back to the Red Lion Inn. He sat quietly, watching Nancy's fitful sleep. There was a pain in her eyes even then that no drug could dull. So she dreamed it over and over, calling out Willie's name, without ever knowing that it really had happened.

"Bill, thank God you've come." This time Nancy's voice was crisp. Her eyes were wide open. Then her gaze shifted back to Willie. She studied his face like a dimly remembered stranger at a class reunion. Willie let go of her hand and slithered backward, out of her line of sight. Addison tensed, waiting for her to point an accusing finger.

"You," she said at last, turning her head to fix him with her stare. "I'm sorry, I can't seem to recall your name. But I know your touch. You were kind to me once. Bill, am I going to die?"

"No," Addison answered emphatically. "Nancy, you were never even sick. The whole thing was a horrible hoax. Those bastards faked the military fever. They fed you drugs to simulate the symptoms. Then they sold you on cryonics and faked your death. It worked because you trusted them. They faked everything except your dream. That was the only thing the drugs couldn't blot out of your memory. You were here all the time. This is where it happened."

Nancy's eyes widened. She shook her head in disbelief.

"Tell her the truth, Willie," Addison snapped.

The look of guilt and misery in his eyes was all the answer Nancy needed.

"You mean it was all for nothing? Bill, all that suffering. Was it just to make somebody rich?"

"If it is any small consolation, my dear, you also contributed mightily to the cause of science. Cryonics will be forever in your debt," Amos Stepp's voice boomed from across the room. "Turn around very slowly and carefully."

Stepp clutched a pistol in both hands. Two men stood poised just behind him. Addison caught a fleeting glimpse of John Victor watching furtively from the doorway.

Nancy saw him too. For a moment it seemed to Addison that she saw no one else, not Stepp or his gun or the guards. Her eyes turned hard and her breath came in short, fast gasps. Addison moved in front of her. The pistol he had picked up almost brushed her face. Her glance fixed on it. She took his hand and squeezed it hard for just a moment.

"Turn around. Turn around or I'll shoot you in the back right now," Stepp ordered. "You, Garvin, you'll be first."

"No," Willie squealed, scuttling to a far corner of the room.

Addison felt Nancy's hand across his stomach. Then her fingers tightened on the pistol in his belt. He turned around slowly with his arms raised, and the gun slid into Nancy's hands.

"They'll get you, Stepp," he said. "They'll find the phony death masks. They'll tie you in to Bundy's murder. Whatever he knew is going to come out sooner or later. Your whole scam is coming apart. You, too, Victor. You're in it just as deep."

Victor faded back into the corridor as though Nancy's eyes had melted him down to a heap of ashes. "It was a con," he said. "I didn't kill anybody. I didn't even know about Bundy. So help me."

"Shut up," Stepp ordered. "Now, move away, Addison, or I might hit your precious Nancy first."

Addison shook his head and walked aside. He braced himself. The blast of a pistol shot rang in his ears. For an instant Amos Stepp appeared truly surprised. He looked down to observe the bloodstain that spread across his chest. His matchstick legs turned to rubber and buckled under his weight. The pistol dropped from Nancy's hand and clattered on the stone floor. Then they heard the first sirens.

A fleet of squad cars clogged the driveway. Addison paused on the porch to observe the swirl of activity. He felt Nancy leaning close against him, her weight resting on his shoulder. John Victor was the last to be led away. If Nancy saw him, she gave no hint of a reaction.

"I love you," she whispered. "You're the only part of this that was ever real. What will they do to Willie? He's such a poor soul."

"He saved your life, Nan. They'll go easy on him."

An FBI agent cradled Rocky lightly under his arm. "This damned thing screwed up television reception for fifty miles," he said as he passed by. "Why the hell would they be stupid enough to leave a piece of gear like this lying around?"

"Stay tuned to your local news," Addison answered. "Nancy Seymour will tell you all about it."